Praise for Adam Wing's
ICARUS

Icarus is a stunning achievement. It retells a tale as old as time, in a way that tears your heart to shreds, yet simultaneously makes it soar. Wing makes this epic Greek myth accessible, while still honoring its antediluvian charm. Admirers of the recent works of Madeline Miller will hold Icarus in similar esteem. Wing's skillful storytelling, combined with his masterful writing talent, make this a book you will not want to miss.

— Chase Connor,
A Surplus of Light

Adam Wing's Icarus is powerful and gripping. It brings life to a myth that always deserved more. Attention to detail and evocative language put you right in the Mediterranean beside iconic characters we all grew up with.

— Matt Berry,
CFEX-FM (X92.9) Calgary

Praise for Adam Wing's published short,
OLD MAN ON THE BUS

*That was both more moving and more terrifying than any horror story
I've ever read.*

– Helen Whistberry,
The Malhaven Mysteries

Also by Adam Wing

Icarus

Apoca Lypse Sink Ships

Old Man on the Bus

MATRIARCH

A Novella
by

Adam Wing

MATRIARCH

Book Cover Design by ebooklaunch.com.

Proofread by Charlie Knight (cknightwrites.com)
Published by Adam Wing.

ISBN
Paperback: 978-1-9995187-5-2
Ebook (ePub): 978-1-9995187-7-6
Ebook (Mobi): 978-1-9995187-6-9

To the doomed.

THE ELDEST

FATE. DESTINY. DOOM.

They rule our lives, decide our futures, queens of fortune and potential. So small are we in Their eyes—so titanic Their vision—we tend to see Them as a single inescapable god, decider of everything, final and first, cause and consequence. But each is unique.

They are Sisters.

Destiny and Fate—the Young Ones—have ever been rivals. Born in the same instant, they squabble for control of all that is and all that will come to pass. They command our stories, vying for ownership. While Fate croons Her songs backward, settling each ending before its start—parables carved in the currents of an immutable universe—Destiny scribbles in the ink of human action, stories born of spirit, courage and resolve, of foolishness, fear and greed. Her endings are those we achieve for ourselves, yet they are no less incvitable, no less *Hers* in the end.

Then there is the Eldest.

Doom.

Doom eclipses Her Sisters. They are nothing that She was not already. Like Fate, She is the chosen endpoint assigned to each living soul; like Destiny, She is the fruit of every worldly ambition. And She is more. Doom is the great and terrible scorecard, the price of admission, deferred until journey's end. She is the reckoning of each life's work, be it arranged in the stars or shaped by choices freely made.

Believe you in Destiny, in Fate, in neither or both, Doom cannot be denied.

She will be there in the end.

Doom awaits us all.

CHAPTER ONE
Doom

EACH Sister was present in the hospital that day. No one saw them. No one heard their voices as they laid claim to the oldest and youngest, to every life and future resting in-between. But they *were* there.

Fate's unyielding certainty clung to the air, mingling with the sharp balm of ammonia hastily spread across vinyl, tile, and plastic. Destiny's resolve crackled around every pulsing body, binding lives in intricate webs of hope, fear, and grim determination. And of course, Doom was there, lurking out of sight, hiding around corners and behind heavy doors. In such desperate settings, where people came to press back against death, fight tooth and nail for one more decade, one more year, just one more breath of life, the Eldest Sister was never far.

Today in particular, however, more than any in a *very* long time, Doom's presence could be felt. Today, she was here with purpose. This was the day the Merrill family

3

would arrive en masse. The day Ayla Merrill, the ancient family matriarch, would come to the hospital to die.

○   ○   ○   ○

"SHE was fine," the man explained—tried to explain—fumbling words as his voice betrayed an agitation barely held in check. "She was normal. Gran's always been—I mean, she's *old*, but she's always been … *healthy*, you know? I can't think of a time I've seen her sick. But she just started coughing and wheezing, and she just—she just … *dropped*. Like a bag of onions!"

"How old is your grandmother?" the admissions nurse asked, pen never leaving her clipboard.

"*Great*-grandmother," the man corrected automatically. "A hundred-nineteen. It's her birthday. It was at her party it happened. Everyone was there. It was something else, really, a miracle—that we could all make it, I mean. Like, not just *most* of us; *everyone* came. So many different schedules. Six generations under the same roof…" The man was beginning to babble. For a time, the nurse allowed him. The patient had been admitted, assigned a bed, and wheeled away by an orderly; it was a slow afternoon, and amazingly, no one else was waiting; no harm letting him unburden himself. Soon she realized, however, if she hoped to get anything useful from him at all, she would to have to interrupt. "…the youngest still poopin' in diapers,

4

of course, but we—" The nurse opened her mouth to cut in.

"Dan!" A female voice slapped at them from the entrance. Five more had appeared through the sliding glass doors. The one who had called out, a well-made-up but dazed-looking young woman—no older than thirty—scooted past a trio of middle-aged ladies supporting a hanging-grey-thread of an eighty—perhaps even ninety—year-old man. "We met up in the parking lot." The younger woman nodded toward the others. "Mum and Dad are right behind. How is she?"

It took the nurse a second to realize this last was directed to her.

"Well, we—"

"Cass! Dan!" A couple in their fifties hurried through the doors and up to the group. "How is she? What do they say?" These questions were *not* addressed to the nurse, who had yet to get a word in.

"I don't know," the young woman, apparently named Cass, answered. "I was just asking."

"I don't know," Dan echoed. Turning back, he resumed his monologue. "She was having trouble breathing, right? Well, first off, she was fine. Everyone was saying…" The man's rambling account washed over her once again. Suppressing the urge to clench her jaw, the nurse watched as three more Merrills trickled in to attach themselves to the

5

group. Was she to contend with the whole extended clan today? she wondered with no small feeling of dread.

Before more could arrive, before Dan could recite the entire family history, she managed to time an interjection into one of his short breaths. The doctors were examining their great-grandmother, she told them—or their grand-mother—or in the case of the ancient-looking man … his *mother*?—the one they called *Gran*, in any case—and they would be back with their diagnosis soon. In the mean time, *no*, they could not *all* go wait with her; *no*, she herself was not going to speculate on what might be wrong, and *yes*, they could remain in the lounge, so long as they kept to themselves and bothered no one.

This last answer was one the admissions nurse would come to regret.

One-hundred-thirty-eight relatives—ninety-nine direct descendants, and a healthy smattering of in-laws—gath-ered in the waiting area that evening. "Gran is a remarkable woman," one of them told the nurse when she approached to suggest electing a contingent that would stay and wait for news, so the others could go home. "Hundred-nineteen and sharper than anyone I know. None of us can imagine what we'd do without her."

"She sounds incredible," she answered. *Now please move on like any normal invasive swarm.*

Eventually, she did convince them. Six would remain through visiting hours. *One* would be allowed to sit overnight with the patient. For this, they elected the young woman, Cass, who had grown up next-door to the old matron. All agreed, she lived closest to Gran's heart.

o   o   o   o

IT was a little after 2 a.m. when Gran awoke. Cass did not immediately notice. Her focus had fallen hard on what the doctor told her, and it was difficult to think of anything else. "It's her time," the woman had said, hands folded on a closed folder containing Gran's entire medical life. "Her body's giving out. She might make it till morning, maybe a day or two, but … she's *very* old."

Old. Cass's laptop sat open in front of her, a half-finished pamphlet design splashed across the dimmed screen. She had hoped to distract herself with work, but for hours she had no more than stared at the open file. …*Might make it till morning, maybe a day or two*… The words circled in her head, overwriting all other thought. …*But she's* very *old*… The idea that this woman, this fixture in Cass's life, would be gone soon, was all she could focus on. As her great-grandmother's sleep became restless, Cass's attention was drawn inward. Even when the old woman slipped back into consciousness, she failed to notice. Only when Gran actually called out, did she finally snap back to the world.

7

"Ollie?" Gran's fear cut the darkness, causing the younger woman to start. "Ollie, where am I? Where is this? What am I doing here? *Ollie*?!"

Tossing her laptop to the other chair, Cass reached for the old woman. "*Sh-hh*, Gran," she whispered. "*Sh-hh-hh*, it's me. It's Cassidy. Your little Cass."

"*Cass*?" If anything, Gran's voice sounded more panicked. "Oh, *God*. Cass … where am I? Where—where's Ollie?"

"Gran, no, it's okay. It's okay. You're in the hospital. You're with me at the hospital. You fainted at the party. We brought you here to rest and get better."

"No. No, I don't like this, Cass. I need to see him. I need … I need … oh…" Her voice trailed off, as though the effort to speak was too much. This frightened Cass. Gran did not scare easily. Gran did *not* get befuddled. She was immutable, a force of nature. Seeing her like this…

"Greatest-Granddad's gone," Cass said, pressing the old woman's knuckles in her palm. "He passed a long, long time ago, remember? Years before I was born. You do, Gran. Don't you?

Surprisingly, this seemed to have a calming effect. Gran's muscles relaxed, and she eased herself back onto the bed. "Yes," she breathed, sounding a little more herself. "Yes, Cass, that's right. A *long* time. I just forgot. Just for a second." She placed a frail hand over Cass's, which Cass then sandwiched in her own. They held on like that

8

for a minute before Gran pulled away. "Poor Ollie," she murmured. "Poor, poor Ollie." Then, "Please, Cassidy, the light. I'd like to see my favourite girl before I go."

Cass flicked the switch on a wall-mounted fixture over the bed, and a dull glow kindled in its frosted bulb. "None of this *before I go* crap," she chided. "You're going to get better, okay? Mum and Dad brought you some things from the house; some clothes, your jewellery, that old book you like to read. They want you to keep your spirits up so you can get out of here and back home where you belong."

Gran smiled. "My little Cass. A hundred-and-nineteen is long enough sentence for anyone, wouldn't you say?" Cass shook her head. Gran had exceeded her generation's life expectancy before she herself was born, yet to her, a world without the old woman in it was unthinkable. "Besides," Gran continued, ignoring Cass's silent objection, "a promise was made many years ago, and I imagine it's time to keep it."

"Gran, what are you—"

"You say they brought my bobbles?"

Sitting back, Cass nodded.

"Please."

Cass allowed herself a moment of uncertainty before retrieving a small cherry-wood box from the windowsill.

The box was an antique. Intricate friezes lay carved around its sides, each depicting a season of the year. Webs of brass and silver decorated the lid, set seamlessly into

9

polished wood. Cass adored this box, though she had never been allowed to touch it, or even look inside. It was strictly off-limits, the only real restriction Gran had ever enforced. Setting it on the old woman's lap, she returned to her chair by the bed.

"I never told you how I ended up with your great-grandfather," Gran remarked quietly, opening the little chest.

Cass took a moment to consider. A legend in the Merrill family—second only to Gran herself—Greatest-Granddad Ollie had died in the 1940s, before even the grandchildren were born. Yet each generation had grown up with him. Sitting cross-legged on the old woman's worn living-room carpet, or curled into an ancient chair or sofa, listening to Gran's stories, they had come to know him, to love him, as if he had always been around. And though his death was something of a murky spot in the family chronicle—rarely discussed and vaguely understood to be suicide—it was his life the old woman loved to recount. The sort of man he was, how much he meant to her. They had gone on such adventures together, lived through incredible events. Through these enthralling tales, Ollie lived again, and the entire family grew to adulate him, even as Gran herself did.

It was no small shock then, when Cass realized she had no idea how Gran had actually come to meet him. *That can't be right. Gran would have told that one. Surely, I would have asked.*

Thinking back, giving herself a good long moment to consider, she found her mind drawing a blank.

Before Cass could voice her surprise, Gran—whose eyes remained fixed inside the box—shot up a silencing finger. "Wasn't a question, Cassidy," the old woman muttered. "I'm not asking; I'm *saying*, you've never heard *this* story."

Cass's mouth snapped shut.

Picking through her jewelry—a bird digging for insects amidst a carpet of fallen nettles—Gran's eyes widened as she spotted what she was looking for. She set the box aside. In her hand remained a silver bracelet formed of fine, interlinking bands. It wore a heavy coat of tarnish, painted on presumably, by time and neglect. It was a wonderfully detailed piece though, and looked to be one-of-a-kind. Cass could not recall ever seeing Gran wear it—or seeing it at all for that matter.

"This bracelet," Gran said, wistfully, "is older than you'd guess. Older than you'd believe, actually. It has more stories in it than I could tell you if I had … well, till you were *my* age. But the most recent, the one as it matters to me—and to *you*—is the tale of your great-grandfather. Oliver. It's a story I've not told anyone. But then, no one as God-awful-old as me could miss how special you are, Cass, could doubt that you deserve to know. I suppose it's time someone does."

Cass's throat seemed to swell. It was a struggle to pull air into her lungs. *She knows she's dying,* she thought. *She knows this will be the last story she tells.* Leaning forward, crushed by the realization, yet desperate to hear what Gran had to say, she listened as the tale began.

"It was, oh … *so* far back now, in Turkey, maybe a year after the war—not the *Great* War; a few years on. After the *Liberation.* I guess these old bones would have looked about your age then—just shy, maybe—a girl, figuring out what it means to be a woman.

The winter rains came strong that year. I don't think I'd seen the river so high…"

WING

CHAPTER TWO
Fateful Bridge

IN all her nineteen years, Ayla had never seen the river this high. Even the bridge back into town looked ready to wash away, the lowest of its three main ropes dropping into the muddy rush, tugging its sisters into a violent, twisting bend.

Her morning had been miserable. The season's figs were only beginning to ripen, and despite having climbed a dozen of the larger trees and combed countless more of the smaller, Ayla had come away with barely enough fruit to be worth the effort. Her satchel sagged forlornly at her hip, no more than a quarter full. Her skin felt chilled and wooden, but she was too drenched to bother keeping the rain off. She was painfully aware of her own feverish pulse thrumming in the nine or ten wasp bites decorating her limbs. So even with the water a foot higher than when she had passed this way at dawn, even with the crossing partially submerged and clearly unsafe, Ayla hesitated not a second before stepping onto the bridge.

13

Father made these ropes, she reminded herself with a confidence she more or less felt. *He's not failed me before. I can trust him one last trip.* If there was anything in the world Ayla could count on, it was her father's workmanship. Stretching a leg onto the swaying line however, feeling it tremble and tug beneath her foot, she conceded that perhaps the danger was greater than she had allowed herself to believe. Perhaps she was so tired, cold, and anxious to get dry, she would actually risk drowning before making the long detour to the other bridge, south of town. Ayla tried to believe this was not the case, though. She preferred to think she was being fearless.

At length, despite a heart-pounding stretch in the middle, when her ankles dipped below the surface and the current threatened to take her, Ayla's confidence proved justified. As she ascended once more toward the far bank, she could almost believe she was going to make it.

Then all ropes shook at once.

Ayla's heart did a somersault. Her foot slipped and splashed down, catching the water like a paddle, nearly tipping her. *A gust of wind*, she told herself, swaying unsteadily as she fought to recover her balance. *Or a piece of debris hitting the line.* Finding her perch once more, she twisted back to look. She cursed aloud. *Oh, what is this, now?*

It had not been a branch or rogue gust of air battering the ropes, but a man who had made his way onto the bridge. He clambered toward her, tugging at the lines as if

14

he meant to steal them. The fibers were slick with rainwater and he was going much too quickly; nearly every other step, one of his feet slipped, all but plopping him into the river. If not for the pinched focus drawn across his brow, Ayla might have mistaken him for a clown, dancing, flailing, tumbling gracelessly in her direction.

The man looked to be foreign. He was pale and flush, with jug ears and a squished, round nose. Garnet-coloured hair lay matted to his brow and chin; were it not soaked, Ayla was certain it would have been a bright, dusty orange. *Englishman*, she thought. *God be good. Aren't we supposed to be free of these invaders?* Seeing he had caught her attention, the man cupped a hand over his mouth and shouted. His words were lost in the storm.

"Get off," Ayla called back. "Wait till I'm across!" Anyone with brain enough for their skull would recognize this bridge was to be crossed one at a time. How had he failed to see this? "*Soldiers*," she breathed. "You'd think the stupid ones would be dead by now." She raised her voice again, though she doubted he would hear any better than she. "Go back! One at a time! One … at … a … *time*!"

She could only guess if her words made it to his ears. Regardless, the man did not turn. He began to wave instead, throwing his arm out over and again, only to lose balance and snatch it back.

What in God's name?

15

Upon the fifth gesticulation, Ayla realized the stranger was in fact pointing, directing her eyes upriver. She sighed; lips pressed together as they were, the sound came out closer to a snort. Careful of her footing, she swivelled around to look. Her mouth fell open at what she saw. Her hands numbed and nearly let go of the ropes.

A tree—a whole old-growth tree, roots and everything—had washed into the river and was bearing toward the bridge. "God be good," she whispered. Turning again to the man, she shouted as loud as she could. "Go back! Go back *now*! *I* can get across but you'll never make it! GO … BACK!"

The stranger shook his head. Whether he was still out of earshot or simply refusing, Ayla could not say. He took another step.

"God, deliver me from idiots." She put her back to him. If she did not move quickly, in a few short minutes, she would be in as much trouble as he.

At last, Ayla's foot crunched onto the bank. She threw herself from the convulsing ropes, her body deflating in a deep gush of relief. Spinning, she saw that the Englishman had nearly made it to the centre of the bridge. She opened her mouth to urge him once more to retreat, but it was too late. The tree was close now, surging right for him. The man made no more attempts to communicate. Nor did he try for either bank. He simply stood facing upriver, watching his doom's approach.

WING

"Why is he just standing there?" Ayla wondered aloud. But did it really matter? She should just go, really. She could do nothing to help the poor idiot; she did not have to stand here and watch him die. Her body resisted any attempt to leave though. She tracked the tree instead, as it reached out with long, crooked branches, devouring the distance between itself and the stranger.

Here it comes.

Ayla could not turn away.

Then, as the wooden behemoth was about to wash through the tiny figure in its path, the man did something wholly unexpected, stealing her breath in the process. Light as a cat, he hopped onto one of the hand-ropes. Before he could lose balance, he threw himself straight out at the tree. The rope released him with a sodden twang. Ayla gasped as he arced into the air.

The tree was seconds away.

High over the water, the man almost looked as if he were flying. For the briefest instant, she imagined he might make it.

He did not.

Splashing into the river, the Englishman just managed to catch hold of the trunk—even as it caught *him* in its fearsome advance. He could not find leverage to pull himself up; it was all he could do to hang on as the tree collided with the bridge. Ropes strained bare seconds before snapping apart, freeing the deadly craft to drag him away downriver.

"Hey!" Ayla called. "Hey, hang on!" If the man let go, she doubted he would surface again for miles. *God protect all idiots.* She wiped a dripping curl from her face. *God, help me rescue this one.* Dropping her figs, she began to run.

Ayla raced the tree down the muddy bank. Her skirt clung to her ankles and thighs, threatening to trip her. Her muscles soon began to burn. Before long, so did her lungs. The man held on, unable to pull himself up, struggling to keep his face above water. *Does he see me coming?* she wondered, snapping through a picket of dead brush. *Is he praying I'll reach him in time? Is he readying himself for God?*

The bank rose into another bluff. This was it, she thought, grasping at weeds as she scrambled up the wet slope. If she was going to risk her life to save this fool, it would have to be here. Atop the rise, she found herself abreast of the tree. Without hesitating, without slowing her stride, she sprinted toward the river.

And she leapt.

Ayla's stomach rose as the ground dropped away. Distance seemed to telescope before her. Her heart threatened to burst. Time congealed around her body, and for a pitched eternity the tree floated motionless below. She held her breath. Hot blood churned within her as the sheen of rainwater and sweat froze against her skin.

WING

Time snapped back into motion, and the tree lunged up like a viper.

Ayla near swallowed her tongue as her feet cleared the crown of roots by cold inches. She landed hard, hugging the bow as she toppled into a skid. A hot wave of scratches and cuts washed up her body, and a woolly musk filled her nostrils. Wet cedar.

She coughed twice and blinked. *I can't believe I just did that.*

The tree was old, thick at its base. Ayla managed to hold purchase as she cautiously found her feet. *God be with me,* she prayed, picking unsteadily through broken branches and limbs. *God, don't let me die saving a foreigner.* The wood beneath her feet shifted with every step, but it did not roll, and she managed to navigate to where the drowning man still clung.

"Good afternoon." The man spoke in Turkish, with an accent she attributed more to his face being halfway underwater than to any particular country.

"Might you—be good enough to—see me out of—this predicame—"

Despite herself, Ayla wanted to laugh. His mouth kept dropping below the surface, forcing him to space out his request, yet he did not sound panicked in the least. By his tone, he might have been asking for directions. His eyes were another matter though. The frenzy in those strange blue orbs was enough to kill any laughter on her lips. It was

19

clear to Ayla, he was every bit as frightened as she. And *she*, she only now realized, was beyond terrified.

"Hold on." She wrapped herself around one of the larger branches and carefully dropped to a crouch—it would not do to pull him out only to fall in herself. The man nodded, watching intently. When she was confident in her perch, Ayla latched a hand to his wrist. "All right," she grunted. "Now, *pull*!"

They worked together. The man kicked frantically. His hand snapped a little higher, and she held it in place, coughing and spitting as water splashed into her mouth. Gradually, his head rose from the surface. Crawling back along the trunk, inch by excruciating inch, Ayla dragged him toward her, until at last they lay head-to-head on the tree, panting and exhausted.

"Thank you," the man gasped. "Thank you … so much!"

"No trouble," Ayla replied breathlessly.

Taking a few seconds to recover, they rose and she led the stranger back toward the bow. "See that turn in the bank?" She pointed ahead of them. "The flow slows on this side. We should be able to jump off. The current's still powerful though, so we mustn't falter. How strong of a swimmer are you?"

A wet breath burst from the man's nostrils. "I can make it."

WING

The moment came, and they jumped. Together, they beat their way to the bank. The Englishman arrived first and reached back to help Ayla. Clinging to one another, they pulled themselves from the water and collapsed on a bed of muddy weeds. For several minutes they lay there.

"Oh, Lord," the man croaked. "Oh, I thought that was it for me."

So did I, Ayla thought. But she said nothing.

At length, the man sat up. Ayla continued to direct her gaze skyward, watching lines of rain expand in prefect circles through her vision. She could feel his eyes on her.

"My name is Oliver Merrill," he said, somewhere to her left. She heard his body shift in her direction, presumably stretching a hand out for her to shake. Swallowing, Ayla pushed herself into a sitting position and turned to face the stranger.

"My name is Ayla." She did not take his hand, offering only a modest nod instead. "Peace be with you."

"Ayla." The man seemed to savour her name on his tongue. By the warmth of his smile, she would have never guessed he had just come a hair's breadth from drowning. "I assure you, the pleasure is mine."

He looked at her with unsettling blue eyes. As if he already knew her. As if he knew something she did not. Those eyes made her nervous.

Ayla wondered if it would have been better to let the river take him.

21

CHAPTER THREE
For Want of a Belt

"YOU wished he'd *drowned*?!" Cass's words cracked the dim room's shadows and spilled into the hall. A perturbed hiccup escaped behind them as she registered just how loud she had been. *Inside voice, dummy.* They were in a hospital after all, and it was the middle of the night.

The old woman had surprised her though. Gran only ever spoke of Greatest-Granddad in the most honeyed terms. His kindness. His courage. Cass would have figured their story to be some kind of fairy tale. Apparently, she was mistaken. "Not love at first sight then," she ventured, lowering her tone to a reasonable hush.

"Oh, it was love," Gran replied, chuckling. "No question. Love *before* first sight, you might say. But I guess I'm getting a bit ahead with that." She allowed herself a second to consider. "Yes, *quite* ahead, I think. If I'm to tell it right, Cass, we'll need to hop back a ways.

"For you to understand what came after the river, or why everything ended up as it did, you'll need to know what brought Ollie to me in the first place, why he thought it could be anything but a fantastically *stupid* idea to crawl onto that bridge. He'd never laid eyes on me, you see. Couldn't have picked me in a lineup of two. Still, I was the reason he was there that day. He had come to town—to that very spot—searching for *me*."

Gran spun the silver bracelet between her palms. Cass regarded it with a strange hypnotized intensity. "But, like I said," the old woman continued, "that's getting ahead. The story begins earlier, at the end of the war. With your Great-Granddad. Oliver.

"Ollie. My Ollie…"

o   o   o   o

THE fight for independence had ended. The Nation of Turkey was born.

British forces, along with the Italians, the French and the Greeks, had begun—and by now, certainly concluded—their withdrawal from the country. Istanbul belonged to the Turks. *Turkey*, after two wars and four years of occupation, once more belonged to the Turks. Cities thundered with patriotic celebration; buoyant spirits shook the buildings and streets. The very winds felt alive with triumph; folks swore they could taste it in the air. Through such delirium, however, amidst spheres gone blind with joy, ghosts lingered in the dark corners and empty beds of

23

countless family homes, in table settings laid out of habit, then hurriedly removed and left bare. The brightest fires of exaltation could not burn away the scars left by the wars that kindled them. And though normality fought to re-assert itself, anger was slow to be abandoned.

It was a dangerous time to be a foreigner in Turkey.

Oliver Merrill had never been one to shy from danger though.

As Lausanne's Quiet descended on the country's last smoldering battlefields, Ollie and his fellow soldiers received a final command from the King. *Come home.* Perhaps alone among his compatriots, he had no intention of following it. Ollie had fallen in love in Turkey—fallen in love *with* Turkey—and he was not ready to let go.

Ollie had never known a world greater than what he could close his eyes and describe by age-eight. Before dropping him into the tail-end of the Great War, life had strayed him no further than Norwich—a bare three hours by train from his London home. In contrast—even as he faced hardship, fear, and death—Turkey seemed a place of magic and wonderment. He came to adore its stories and its food, its music and its art. And above all, its people. "Gone native," he heard his comrades whisper now and again, because he spent so much time out in the city. It was intended as a slight, but he wore the phrase with pride. Ollie wished he *could* go native, shed his English persona and live life as a Turk.

If only he had not been at war with the very people he so admired.

Now the wars were over. Ollie was free to explore the country without fear of being killed, without having to kill anyone else. Go home? He could as easily have left a leg or an arm—even an eye—behind him in the dirt. And though he knew one day he would set it all aside and return to England, so did Ollie know, that day was ahead of him.

So, when Sts George's, Patrick's and Andrew's Crosses—along with their flapping field of blue—were drawn for the last time from their brass seat above the erstwhile capital, Ollie was nowhere to be found. Heavier his final month's wages, he had long since slipped from the city. The King's Armies would have to make their way home without him; Ollie's journey was on a different path. Through a land he had only known as trespasser, as *enemy*. A land he was determined to make it his friend.

An irresistible challenge.

And indeed, it *was* a challenge. Even smaller towns and villages frequently met Ollie with stonehearted enmity. As often as not, he was run out of town the moment he opened his mouth to reveal himself. As often as not, with a gnarling dog or two snapping at his calves. But not always. Many places accepted him. Some begrudgingly, some with a sincerity to bolster his tired spirit. Whenever one did, Ollie worked to inject himself into the community. He sat with old-timers, drawing honeyed smoke from nargiles and expelling it in fragrant clouds, listening to embellished stories of youthful indiscretion—and doing his best to entertain them with tales of his own. He laughed beside mothers and wives, as they laughed at him for begging to help with the evening meal—for insisting they teach him to make soup as delicious as theirs.

When his money ran out, Ollie found work where he could. He farmed and he fished, he hammered, sawed, and shovelled—ditches, wells and stables alike. Trading a pocket watch his sister gave him for a 1903 Ottoman Mauser rifle, he learned to hunt halal so he could barter with rabbits, birds and deer he encountered between towns— or simply eat them as it suited him. His clothes wore thin and his hair grew long, yet Ollie saw more of the country and its people than he had dreamed possible as a soldier. He made, and said farewell to, countless friends he knew he would never see again. And one or two enemies.

As Ollie travelled, however, he was surprised to observe a subtle loneliness making its home in the hollow beneath his ribs. He found himself craving deeper, more enduring companionship, the kind of connection one simply did not find on the road. Yet for whatever reason, he could not allow his legs to rest. Stops rarely lasted more than a few days—never longer than a week or two. One moment he was surrounded by friendly faces; the next, he knew it was time to move on. This happened over and again. No matter where Ollie was, or what time of day, he found his eyes drifting toward the horizon, seeking something just beyond its bounds. He was searching, he realized. This was why he could not go home after the war. He was looking for ... *something*. Until he could satisfy his search, stopping was wholly impossible.

It was late autumn when he arrived at the place he would find what he was looking for.

Making his way through the rugged hills beneath the North Anatolian Mountains, Ollie spotted a small sheep farm in the valley below. The weather was fine; he had plenty of supplies—even a little money—and the sun had not yet peaked in its path across the sky. There was no need to stop. His bones ached—walking so much, they *always* ached—but people hardly ever shot at him anymore, and he could not help feeling cheerful. *March on, soldier*, he directed when the little cluster of buildings fell into sight. *Too early still for a rest.*

So he thought, at least. Fate had made other plans. On this day, it manifested in the form of a frayed strip of cloth.

For years, Ollie's regulation suspenders had served King and Country. Steadfast in their duty, they endured as he fought, crawled, ran, and on occasion even danced, in service to the Crown, stretching a little longer, wearing a little thinner with each passing day. Until today. Today, their task would prove too great. After a brief squat in the bushes, as Ollie slipped the fraying straps back over his shoulders, by the strain of one last tug, they gave in to the inevitable, snapping apart in his surprised finger.

They had been his only pair.

This was a problem. Long daily treks and occasional stretches of fasting saw Ollie much leaner than the well-fed soldier whose clothes he still wore. Continuing without *something* to keep his trousers up no longer appeared to be an option. Hand agrip to his now-drooping waistband, he halted to consider the farm still hovering in the lowest corner of his vision. Perhaps it was a *perfect* time for a rest.

This was how he came to know Tansel and Dursun.

Their farm was a meagre affair, on a tract of land nestled in a tiny hill-ringed basin. While not exactly destitute, the old couple was as far from wealthy as two people with full bellies could rightly claim. They certainly had no extra suspenders to give wayward strangers in ill-fitting clothes. They were kind however, and happy to offer what help they could. "I might have some old scraps of leather in the barn," Dursun said. "I can make you a belt."

Ollie accepted. He wished to pay, but they would not allow it. "Stay the night as our guest," Tansel insisted. "Pay us with your company." So Ollie stayed.

They fed him the best meal he had eaten in months, then Tansel folded him into a chair—almost forcefully— and gave his hair and beard a much-needed trim. He slept in the barn, and in the morning, his new belt was ready. Again, Ollie tried to give them money, and again they shook their heads. He insisted they at least let him help with some chores before he moved on. An offer he knew no farmer would refuse.

After a rewarding day's labour, at his hosts' behest, Ollie stayed another night.

Two nights became a week, which stretched on for nearly three months. Ollie kept expecting his feet to once more begin to itch, but they never did. The restlessness that had tracked him across this country seemed to have finally lost his trail. This was the existence, these were the people, he had imagined he would find in his travels. For the first time in his life, Ollie felt content.

He would have stayed longer—years perhaps—believing he had at long last found his elusive *something*. But once again, fate took a hand.

One morning, as Ollie he swung the barn door open and stepped into the yard, he beheld a sight to fill his heart with foreboding. A sheep had been attacked in the night, ripped to pieces, and partially carried off. Torn-out innards and grim confetti of wool, skin and meat lay littered over a wide patch of earth. Spilled blood muddied the ground around it. Ollie was no stranger to carnage, but the ferocity displayed in the remains, the violence with which it had been slaughtered, was enough to shake him.

When he summoned Dursun and Tansel, their reactions were nearly as alarming as the sheep itself. They were devastated of course—the loss of a single animal was a grievous blow—but Ollie saw no confusion or surprise on their faces. They surveyed the carnage in silence. And they exchanged a look.

They know what's caused this, he thought.

They've seen it before.

CHAPTER FOUR
Tale of a Thief

"WOLF."

Ollie considered the possibility.

A wolf? No, I don't think so.

The carnage he had found that morning, and then spent much of the day disposing of, could have easily been caused by some kind of large predator—say, a wolf—but that did little to explain the fence. Eight feet high and built solid, it was barrier enough for just about anything. Yet the gate was latched when he checked it, and there were no broken slats or holes dug out beneath. And as far as carrying so much of the carcass back over again, well … a tiger or a leopard maybe, not a wolf.

Yet, that was what Tansel said—*wolf*—her eyes unclouded by doubt.

It was the first word either she or her husband had given the subject all day. In the morning, after staring at the bloody debris in silence, they had turned and walked back into the house, Dursun first then Tansel a few minutes

31

after. When Ollie brought it up later, each of them simply continued whatever chore they were engaged in and suggested his time would be better spent doing the same. Only at supper, after harassing them with his own speculations, did he finally put a crack in their silence.

"How'd it get in, I wonder?" Ollie had said, ripping a chunk of bread to dip into his red lentil soup. "Beastie'd need a ladder and grapple to hop *that* fence." Tansel stiffened. Refilling Ollie's tea, she accidentally splashed some over the lip of his cup. Setting down the pot, she shared a look with her husband. Neither offered a reply. "For that matter," he went on, pretending not to have noticed, "how'd it get out again, dragging a whole half-sheep back with it? What on God's Green Earth could have managed *that?*"

The question hung over them like the warm smells of their food. Dursun, whose spoon had been halfway to his lips, closed his mouth and set down the utensil. Troubled eyes lingered on his bowl. Tansel took up her own spoon. Moving with such calculated poise that both men's focus—along with every point of tension in the room—shifted momentarily to centre inexorably onto her, she dipped into her broth and blew a wisp of steam from the hot liquid. Her gulp, when she swallowed, was nearly as loud as the preceding quiet. She met Ollie's perplexed gaze, and she spoke the word.

Wolf.

Her voice sounded strangled, as if some broth had stuck in her throat.

Ollie waited. *There must be more. If they're this scared, this sure about what's happening, it can't be some run-of-the-mill, everyday sort of forest prowler.* And again, there was the fence. He had managed to open the subject now, though; he knew he would soon learn the truth.

Sure enough, when Dursun spoke next, it was in the foggy cadence he used to begin his stories—the old farmer, Ollie had learned, was a consummate storyteller. "In these parts, we call him Erbörü," he said quietly. "He's lived in our hills since before my grandfather was a boy."

Ollie shifted in his chair. His Turkish was far from perfect, but he was fairly confident *Erörü* meant *werewolf.*

Now that he had begun, Dursun quickly fell into the tale, the natural rhythms of the telling overriding any initial reticence. "My father's voice was the first I heard speak the name. *Erörü.* I was young then, and he liked to scare me to sleep at bedtime." The farmer's eyes wrinkled slightly at the memory. "That was many years ago. 'Erörü was a man once,' Father said, 'like you or me … only different in one vital way. *He* was a man without honour. He was a *thief.*

"'Yes, once upon a time, Erörü was a villain, a true scoundrel, but God be good, he was an *extraordinary* thief. He could steal your horse from between your legs, and you'd ride five miles in an empty saddle before noticing it gone. He was greedy, and above all, cruel. If he entered

33

your home one night and made off with your good dishes, you could be sure he'd be back the next for the silver to go with them. Night after, he'd have your wife's jewels; another still and he'd winnow out where you stashed your gold. If you thought to stay awake, stand guard and catch him, your *bed* would be gone in the morning! If you set a trap for him, *he stole the trap*! Oh yes, Erbörü was the *best* of thieves … and the *worst* of men. By the time he finished with you, you'd call it lucky if your house had all its walls.'

"So said my father."

Ollie leaned forward in his chair, eyes on the near-invisible smile tugging at Dursun's lip.

"Well, it happened," the old farmer went on, "that Erörü—though no one called him that then, as he was still a man—grew tired of stealing from farmers and merchants. Their dusty-dull valuables and sad, gaunt purses, their piddly heirlooms. Their food. It all felt so … pedestrian. Don't get me wrong; never in his life did he feel a twinge of remorse, no matter how poor his victims, or how little he left them in the end. He just wanted better loot for his efforts.

"So, he decided to rob a prince.

"Beneath God's watchful eye, Erörü travelled to the governing prince's palace, slipping in unseen to see what treasures he would find. And I can tell you, treasures he found! In a few short hours, he was skulking out with more wealth than he'd seen in his entire thieving career. Everything he'd hoped for and more!

"But as I said, this thief's greed knew no bounds. One night's takings could never satisfy—no matter how great the bounty—so he returned the following evening. And again, the next night. There was just so much; Erbörü couldn't stop! Night after night, he slithered back to the palace to pilfer whatever he could lay his hands on, filling his hidden lair with enough treasure to feed a town for three-hundred years.

"On the seventh night, his fortunes turned. He was captured by the palace magician who set a curse on him, transforming him into the animal of his heart, a wolf as black as night. Before the thief knew what happened, he was cast from the palace to live or die as a slavering beast!" Dursun tossed back the last of his tea and slapped his cup on the table. This earned an irritated frown from Tansel.

"Unfortunately," he continued, seemingly oblivious to his wife's reproachful look, "on two legs or four, Erörü remained a most accomplished thief. And though he dared not return to the palace for fear of the magician, he took his revenge on the people of these hills. His animal brain no longer cared for gold, ivory, or shiny rocks. He took their *animals*. Their sheep and their goats, their cattle and their chickens. Even, sometimes … their children.

"'Be a good little boy and lie still,' Father would whisper." Dursun's aspect seemed to soften when he mentioned his father, his eyes grow wistful—a rare mien on the kindly but austere sheep farmer. But as he continued, the hint of a smile faded, first from his eyes, then his lips. "That's what he said. 'Lie still and be quiet or Erbörü will steal you away and eat you!' Scared me near to death! I never really believed, of course. Not until I was older…

"I was thirteen when the wolf came to my uncle's farm. It was just like today, a sheep savaged overnight, a good part of its carcass taken. The next night it was one of his dogs—simply gone this time, only a splash of blood in the grass to mark its struggle. Another animal the next night, and two more after that. Just like the thief in Father's stories.

"I arrived with my parents on the fifth day; the whole family had gathered by then. To us kids it was an adventure, but the adults wore grim faces. They knew too well how it would end."

Dursun paused. The food was gone, and Tansel, having cleared the bowls and flatware, portioned out the last of the tea. The older man took a sip, grimaced at the bitterness, then reached for his tobacco. He wanted to appear to be ordering his mind, Ollie thought, but as the farmer raised a match to the decorated wood bowl of his pipe, the younger man noted its flicker over visibly shaking fingers.

"Every night, well after the sun's last ray had melted from the sky, Erörü returned to slaughter another of my uncle's beasts. Sometimes two or even three. We built a

36

new, taller fence. We set traps. We laid in wait with our rifles. But he was like a ghost. No fence could keep him out; no trap would snare him. We ran out of bullets after the first week. He never did come for the children, thank God—I suppose my father embellished that bit—but it was like living in a nightmare, even so. We greeted each morning with a new death, a new stain of crimson in the pasture.

"For twenty-one days, we watched my poor uncle's livelihood erode away. Night after night, Erbörü appeared from the dust, *killed*, then melted like a shadow in the sun. We were helpless. My father, a brave man—God rest his soul—but a famously foolish one, hid among the flock one night, hoping to catch the beast close-up and put an arrow through his neck. He was injured in the attempt and lucky to escape.

"Three long weeks. Then we gave up. Uncle released what was left of his animals—his dogs, his chickens, and his goats—everything still breathing. None would survive if he kept them; maybe on their own, some might make it away…"

Tapping ash into the brass dish in front of him, Dursun lifted his cup for another sip, only to find it empty. He set it back down, then absently tipped it sideways onto the table. It rolled a three-quarter circle on its bottom compass before Tansel snatched it up again. She laid a slap on her husband's arm—more habit, Ollie thought, than actual reprimand—before setting it upright.

Ollie flicked one of his last cigarettes into his mouth and lit it. He offered another to Tansel, who he knew appreciated an occasional after-supper smoke but hated the click of a pipe between her teeth. Not tonight though; she declined with a shake of her head. "And this *Erbörü*," he said, not quite ready to credit Dursun's story, "you actually saw him? You *watched* him appear out of nowhere, then … disappear?" As he spoke, Ollie realized he was already working up a plan to kill such a beast. Ever the soldier, he could not but approach the situation tactically. Which was not to say he believed they had been visited by a werewolf…

Dursun nodded. "We all saw him, yes—especially Father; he got a *very* close look. But only I caught Erörü's secret. I told my family; God knows, I tried. But I was young, and few cared to hear me. It was too late anyway. Uncle released his animals the next day."

"Secret?"

Dursun shook his head. "I don't know; maybe they were right. It was so long ago, and I was very young. Maybe I didn't see what I thought."

Ollie waited. It was Tansel who finally answered. "Erörü does not jump tall fences." She stood grim-faced behind her husband, resting a hand on his care-sloped shoulder. "He does not pass through them like a ghost, as some claim. He *flies*. He dives into the pen like a hawk. *This is what my husband saw that night.*"

Dursun gave Tansel's fingers a squeeze. "It's true. Too often I doubt, but in my heart, I know what I saw. Happening to glance up on that last terrible night, I spotted a strange shadow pass over the moon. I tracked the shape across the sky—my eyes were sharp as anything back then—and watched as it slowed then stopped above us. It was him; I knew it. But my voice had fled. Try as I might, I could not call out. And then he fell.

"When Erbörü finished with the sheep or goat—or whatever life he took that night—when he disappeared once more, I looked up and saw his shape again, shrinking away between stars."

Ollie leaned back in his chair. *Well, that sure was a story*, he thought, exhaling smoke and feeling thoroughly sated. Did he believe it though? He could not say for sure yet. He continued to listen as it drew to a close. Dursun spoke of Erörü returning four more times in his life, devouring whole flocks, ruining livelihoods. Neither he nor Tansel had known those families, but word spread fast in these hills. The accounts were chillingly similar.

"It would appear," Tansel finished when her husband's melancholy had finally stripped him of his voice, "God has permitted the wolf to show himself again. And this time, it is *we* who are fated to lose." She examined the spent leaves at the bottom of her cup. The words fell heavy from her mouth, drawing an even heavier silence behind them.

It was Ollie's turn to break it.

"I daresay *not*!" The old couple jumped at his outburst. Ollie thumbed out his cigarette. Maybe he *could* accept the idea of an ancient flying werewolf; it was conceivable, at least. What he could *not* accept was the despair he was seeing in his friends. "No, Dursun, this wolf of yours may have seemed an impossible foe when you were a boy, but you're grown now, a man who already knows its secret. *And you've got a stalwart of the British Empire at your side!*"

He pushed his chair back and stood, pressing his fists into the table.

"No, Tansel, it's not you—not *we*—who are fated to lose. Not this time. Not tonight, or tomorrow, or night after that. We are the ones who will *stop* this monster! I promise you!"

His hosts regarded him in wonderment. He could see his conviction drifting across the table, percolating into them. He watched it pool in the depths of their tired eyes.

"We are going to put an end to this wolf," he avowed in a low voice that brooked no dispute, "to this vile thief! Tonight. *This* night! Once and for all!"

The silence that followed held none of the doubt or dread of those that came before. Only fierce determination.

WING

<u>CHAPTER FIVE</u>
Wolf's Blood

OLLIE pushed back at the swell of fatigue threatening to engulf him. His limbs felt sluggish, his eyelids weighted. Clasping lashes drew together, knitting into a pair of singular dark lines. He snorted and gave his head a shake. Keeping watch—not falling asleep on watch—was a skill he had gained in His Majesty's service, but no matter how practiced he had become, it was ever a miserable chore.

The night was clear at least, stars so dense he could scarcely make out the serpentine void between them. *More like splintered daylight*, he thought. If by some unlikely miracle Dursun's story proved true, he would have no trouble spotting the wolf against such a backdrop. Though, really ... what were the odds of that happening?

Who's to say, a voice in Ollie's head challenged.

Any reasonable person, he replied silently. *There are no such things as werewolves.*

Well, something made it over the fence. Something killed that sheep. If you don't believe Dursun, why are you even out here?

41

Ollie cleared his throat. Cradling his Mauser rifle, butt and barrel, he returned its sight to the pen, some three-hundred yards below. "Dursun and Tansel are fine people," he muttered to the bushes and weeds. "I've come to love them both. But in this instance—and I'm not saying they're lying, or-or off their rocker or anything—but *in this instance*, I'd suggest they may be peddling some top-market sheepshit."

Then what do you *think happened?*

Ollie scowled. Incredulity aside, he could divine no better explanation for what had occurred. So, with a sense of bleak irony—because he prided himself a reasonable person—he had to consider the possibility. And as closely as he watched the sheep pen itself, Ollie directed one eye toward the heavens.

The night drew on. A cool breeze blew past him and down into the vale, carrying scents of fir trees and wet grass. The hillside shivered as if in anticipation. It had been an age since Ollie lay in ambush, but he recognized the familiar tensions as they settled in. Dursun was on the rocky slope across from him, he knew, ready with his own rifle. No doubt, the farmer was having an easier time staying awake; as far as Ollie could tell, he slept no more than an hour or two each night. Ollie was the better shot though. He would need to be at his best tonight; he could not lose focus.

If only the ground were a little less cold.

And a lot dryer.

Dawn's first light was a distant dream when the target appeared. Ollie spotted it a half-mile out, not even a shadow yet, just a dint in night's layered crystal surface. *Could be a bird*, he told himself stubbornly. Whatever it was, it was big. And moving in their direction. He lifted his Mauser to track it in the sight.

The speck was in no hurry. It moved slowly, lazily, as if drifting on the wind—only the wind blew against it. Had the old man spotted it too? he wondered. Did seeing it return him to those terrible weeks in his youth? Ollie watched as the tiny dot grew into a shadow, then the shadow began to take shape. He could not say with absolute certainty what he was looking at, but he had a pretty good notion. Four limbs. Bushy tail. Wedge-shaped head. No beak. No wings. No ruffling feathers to speak of.

A flying wolf.

He blinked once. Then again. It would not have been his first time seeing things on watch that were not actually there. The mind liked to play its tricks. But typically, he was up for days before anything like that started to happen. No matter how he shook his head or blinked, the strange vision remained.

So Ollie allowed himself a moment to re-frame the universe.

"All right," he said aloud, accepting that such a thing could exist. "Erbörü it is, then."

WING

The creature arrived some minutes later. It did not strike right away, but strayed a broad circle above the farm, like a vulture over a dying animal. Even as Ollie craned his neck to watch it, he leveled his Mauser to the pen below. "We must wait until he's on the ground," Dursun had asserted earlier in the night. "Only God knows how fast the monster can fly. If we miss, he may disappear before we get a second shot." Ollie had disagreed. He would hit it, he had insisted. Better to not risk another sheep. Better not to fire into the chaos of a panicked flock. But the farmer had been adamant, and as the stakes were his, so was the decision. For the moment, Ollie held his shot.

Erbörü's path began to constrict, gradually at first but faster and faster as he circled toward centre. The beast was preparing to dive. Ollie dropped his eyes bare moments before he fell. Any resemblance to a bird quickly vanished. The wolf did not settle to the ground as a vulture does, then sally up to claim his dinner; he did not strike down like a hawk, snatching his prey in a powerful death-grip. He dropped, rather, in a long, almost lazy arc, accelerating as he neared the earth. He was running when he touched down—inside the pen and faster than Ollie would have thought possible.

I said I'd wait till he's on the ground. He aligned his weapon's sight and pressed a finger into the cradle of its trigger. *Didn't say a thing about letting him make a kill.* Before he could finish this thought, Dursun's rifle called out from across the vale.

Erbörü did not stumble or slow. The farmer had missed.

Less than a second had passed but the flock was already registering the wolf's presence. In another, it would be too late. Ollie exhaled half a breath and set his sight ahead of the sprinting beast. Erbörü's steps shortened as he reared toward his prey.

The wolf lunged.

Ollie fired.

The Mauser's report cracked the night. Erbörü stumbled sideways and skidded into the dirt, an orange burst erupting from his shoulder, a jet of flame spearing out from dark fur. *Trick of the light*, Ollie thought, ejecting the spent shell and snapping his bolt to load another. But then … there was only starlight, crystal and cold. Nothing like the blazing flare his eyes insisted they saw. Perhaps the bullet ignited the beast's fur? Was that possible?

Erörü scrambled up. A pool of what were clearly flames sprouted from the ground where he had fallen, dripping from the wound in his side. The creature was *bleeding* fire, a detail even Dursun's story—fanciful as it was—had overlooked.

Changes nothing. Ollie raised his sight again.

Before he could get another shot, Erörü was up, flinging himself back into the air.

WING

The leisurely pace was gone. Dursun, it seemed, had been right; the wolf was capable of *much* greater speeds. The glowing wound in his side cut a coral streak across the night's starry sheath.

No time to think. Scrambling up on legs all but gone numb, Ollie hurried down the rough slope. The farmer would be rushing in as well, he knew. Only one of them could go after the wolf, and Ollie was determined for it to be him. The old man was liable to get himself killed.

He did not wait when he arrived at the lopsided little stable, but darted in and saddled Kiz, the farm's only horse. Dursun appeared just as Ollie was throwing a leg over the animal's back. "Don't be a fool," he said. His words were clipped, his voice pleading. "Alone and at night, it's too dangerous!"

"Not much for it," Ollie answered. "The trail won't last." Before the other man could reply, he dug his heels into the horse's flanks and was out the stable door, rushing past the pen where tongues of fire still licked the night air. It had rained in the afternoon so there was little fear of the flame spreading. *Lucky us.*

Eyes skyward, Ollie could still make out the wound burning in Erbörü's side, an orange comet flickering in the distance. Before long, even that would disappear. But the wolf was hemorrhaging fire now, leaving a trail of light on the ground behind him. Ollie could follow it all the way to his den. *You're mine,* the young soldier silently avowed.

46

MATRIARCH

Whatever you are, however you came to be, I won't let you bring ruin to my friends!

WING

<u>CHAPTER SIX</u>
The Den

GRAN emptied her water cup and set it down. Smacking her lips, she quivered around a dainty, old-lady cough. Cass waited for the story to resume. For a time, her great-grandmother said nothing. She appeared to be weighing the younger woman in the corner of her eye.

Here we go.

For as long as Cass could recall, Gran had delighted in telling fantastical stories she swore to be true, baiting her audience with impossible events until someone inevitably voiced a doubt—and she *always* got someone to bite. Usually Cass. Then she would turn it around, explaining things differently, or adding a detail to show, not only could it be true, it probably *had* to be—no matter how implausible it had at first seemed. It was the old woman's favorite game. Surely, this was what she was doing now, Cass thought.

'Bullshit,' I'll say. 'You're making that up!' And then … I don't know, somehow, it'll make sense, and I'll look stupid.

Still, this one was a doozy. Werewolf? Of course, there was no such thing. Certainly, not a flying one. *Certainly*, not a flying one with fire blood!

Cass exhaled a throatful of gravel. *Dammit.*

"So…" she began tentatively, "that was how it really … *actually* happened? I mean, you weren't there, right? Great-est-Granddad *told* you all this. So, how sure are you…" Gran leveled a look at her, face puckered at the doubt in her voice. And there was that mischievous twinkle. Right on schedule

Got me again, Gran.

Then Cass saw something else, concealed behind the impish light in the old woman's eyes. A shark's silhouette below a laughing, splashing swimmer. Even as she gasped, certain she had never observed such a look before, she realized it felt familiar. Like it had always been. Like it was a part of Gran, invisible for want of absence.

Anger? Was that it? *Almost…* Her mind constricted around the aberrant, barely impressed feeling, struggling to name it. Then it came. *Oh my God.*

Fury.

Cass's eyes widened as the word formed spontaneously in her head. *Holy shit.*

She could feel it now, waves of violent intent roiling toward her through deep-funnel pupils. She tried to swallow but choked on her tongue. Her chair groaned as she staggered to her feet. "I—um…" she croaked. "Here, let me

49

refill your water. And I … I—" Words fought to escape; her throat seemed to close around each syllable. "—should have a sip myself."

Leaving the cup, Cass grabbed the empty carafe beside the bed, and with a few mumbled words, staggered into the hall.

"What was *that*?" she demanded in a querulous whisper, hurrying up the empty corridor. "Holy shit, Cassidy. Get it together!"

She set the carafe into a dispenser by the nurses' station and depressed the blue button to fill it. A crystal finger streamed into the vessel, sighing as it pattered against the plastic bottom. Focussing on that cool pillar of water, Cass allowed her nerves to settle.

It was not the look in her great-grandmother's eyes that had bothered her—she had already dismissed this as a trick of the light, or … or … her mind playing games—it was that she could believe she saw it at all. "Silly," she said aloud, rubbing her eyes as the water level rose. "Stupid." *I really don't know what I was thinking.*

Gran was waiting when she returned. Gran. Wonderful Gran, who she had known all her life. No fury, no blaze of violence, only the spirited old woman everyone loved. There had been no *look*, just Cass's own imagination. Thoroughly embarrassed, Cass splashed some water into the cup, took a quick sip, then set it back on the tray. *Stupid.*

WING

Gran glanced at the water. At Cass. She nodded thoughtfully then parted her lips to speak. "So, you think maybe it didn't happen the way I said?" She squeezed her mouth into a perfectly straight line. *To hide her grin*, Cass thought, pressing herself to engage in the old woman's game—and forget the look she had most definitely imagined. "Is that what you're insinuating? Maybe Greatest-Granddad made it up? And that makes me *what*? A gullible idiot?" Cass tried to object, but Gran quickly overrode her. "You think because I'm old, I can't tell what's real, young lady? You think you can, with your *emails* and your *youtubes*?" She waved a dismissive hand at Cass's laptop sitting closed in the other chair.

Cass swallowed and relaxed. This was how it was supposed to go. This was the Gran she knew. And she had *definitely* been baiting her. "It's not the same," she half-heartedly argued. "Computers are just tools. They have no say in whether something's true or not. Or whether you believe it." As she spoke, she noted this was not actually the case. How many friends and colleagues accepted any old thing they read online? But Cass had no desire to make her great-grandmother's point for her, much less explain click-bait to the hundred-nineteen-year-old dying woman. Instead, she went on the offensive. "You're talking about a *magical monster* though, Gran! Flying wolf? *Fire blood*? I think a little doubt could be called reasonable."

Gran chuckled and licked her lips. She had abandoned any effort to suppress her smile. Cass exhaled. *Here it comes.* Defeated, but in good spirits, she leaned in, wiping her palms on her leggings.

The old woman's attention returned to the item in her hands. "When Great-Granddad Ollie caught up to Erbörü, he found the wolf wearing this." Her smile faded. She thumbed the bracelet one last time before holding it out. "Try it on."

Cass took it. It was smaller than she had initially thought. Much smaller. Was it even a bracelet? Whose wrist would fit such a thing? A child's ... maybe. *Wait, did Gran just say Ollie'd found this on the wolf?* How big did wolves' legs get, anyway? Whatever it was—wherever it came from—it was not going to fit *her.* Not even Gran, with her shrunken wrists, could have worn the thing. "This—" Cass stammered, "I—it's... This won't fit."

"Just try."

Cass sighed. How had she failed to notice how tiny this thing was, anyway? Pursing her lips, she poked a digit through the silver loop. Not quite small enough to be a ring, but not that far off. *No prob,* she thought, mildly amused. *Just four more to go.* She squeezed her fingers together, making a display of pushing them into the bracelet. The metal was rough with tarnish and warm against her skin. It slid up her fingertips, past her knuckles, and over the slope of her thumb.

WING

Somehow—though she could not *begin* to guess how—it fit.

Cass examined her arm. The silver band had not appeared to stretch or grow in any way, yet it was now the exact size of her wrist. It was just suddenly … on.

Incredible.

Before she could begin to marvel at this, something even more remarkable stole her attention. Overcome with a sudden sense she was falling, Cass lurched back in place. Her chair slipped out from beneath her. She scrambled to catch it, but her hands closed on air. Her thighs, her butt, her whole *self*, rose from the cradle of her seat. Still bent as if sitting, she found herself freed from gravity's pull. She was floating, hovering in the air.

Flying. Holy hell, I'm flying! Cass voiced her astonishment in what were meant to be words, but came out closer to a stunned, inhuman squawk.

Gran nodded. "So you are, my dear," she said, correctly interpreting the younger woman's sound. "And I think you'll find you can control it. So, if you'd be so kind as to fly back into your seat, I'd like to finish my story. The doctors say I haven't long, you know."

Alight with wonder, Cass cast her eyes across the room—she was practically on the ceiling! Then her great-grandmother's words gradually filtered into her brain. With a measured breath, she swallowed her amazement.

WING

Dropping back into her chair—she *could* control it—she leaned forward. "This is how he flew, isn't it? The wolf? Er— Erbooru? He was wearing this, you said." She flashed the bracelet at the old woman. Gran just smiled. "Okay Gran, I guess I believe you. Holy shit—I mean, after that, I kind of have to. Right?"

Gran snorted. "I should hope so. Now, may I continue?" Cass nodded, trying hard to focus on her words—a tall order after what she just experienced. But her great-grandmother was an expert storyteller, and it did not take long for her to capture Cass once more.

"Poor Ollie," she muttered. "He tracked the blighted wolf all that night…"

o   o   o   o

OLLIE dared not move too quickly. The terrain was uncertain and all but invisible in the dark. The risk of Kiz tripping and throwing him—or worse, breaking a leg—was too great. Yet the trail grew colder by the minute—quite literally—as bright liquid markers burned themselves out. Come morning, he wagered, the fires would be so small, so dim in the daylight, they would be near impossible to spot. If they still burned at all by then.

The sky, unfortunately, remained indifferent to Ollie's concerns. As the hanging scree of stars sank back into the purple-black mire that surrounded them—which itself grew paler each time he raised his head to look—he found himself squinting just to catch sight of the next burning flicker. Night's march into day had begun. One way or another, the game would soon be up.

Maybe wounding him will have done the trick. Maybe just the pain of getting shot will be enough to keep him away. He would have loved to believe this; somehow, he knew better. If he failed to kill the wolf tonight—or today rather, he supposed, watching the last stars fade away overhead—Erbörü would almost certainly return. *Only, he'll be cautious now. He'll be ready for any ambush we set.* As was so often the case in his experience, it would have to be now. Or it was going to be never.

To Ollie's relief, the trail at last came to an end. None too soon too, as vails of sooty light had already begun to claw at the horizon. He found himself at a stone ruin, deeply weathered and half sunken into the earth. An ancient manner, he guessed, or a long-forgotten mosque. Such lonely places lay hidden in glades and shadowy alcoves up and down these hills, last remnants of abandoned settlements, most—this one included—little more than worn piles of rock.

A wreath of embers dappled the ground where Erbörü had circled the site—on foot, judging by recently trampled brush. Ollie could see no trail leading back out. *Still here then. Probably has a den somewhere inside. Might even be asleep by now ... or waiting out of sight ... setting an ambush of his own.*

WING

Ollie was no stranger to death. He had seen it fall on friend and foe alike. On more than a few adrenaline-wrought occasions, he had been the one to deal it. Through it all, he had come to a significant realization: in battle, there were no such things as heroes, and there were no cowards. You followed orders, and you made it through however you could. Valour was surviving to tell the tale. Courage was coping with terror beyond your control. He reminded himself this as he cut a wide path toward the southern perimeter—downwind of the ruin—and dismounted as quietly as he could.

No cowards.

No heroes.

Do what you must and come out alive.

The thought did little to assuage his fears. It never helped much.

Predawn light drizzled through a ridgeline of frosted grey clouds. Breaths of rain filtered the atmosphere into a fine, chilled mist as Ollie stepped toward the ancient pile of stones. Gusting air tugged his clothing in an attempt to draw him back, away from this dangerous place. The heap lay deathly still in front of him, too many shadows among its rocks, too many places for a wolf to hide. He could feel his skin constrict against the chill.

Drawing closer, Ollie spotted an opening—what must have once been a doorway but had collapsed into a crooked little warren—so low, a person would have to crouch to enter. A carpet of cinders lay sprinkled before it. A welcome mat of sorts, inviting him in.

Erbörü's lair.

He ducked forward, dropping to one knee, and aimed his rifle inside. He could discern no movement. No wolf leapt out to open his throat. For all he knew, Erbörü lay not ten feet ahead of him though, invisible in the dim. Twin hammers beat an angry rhythm in his chest. He squinted, pressing his vision into the darkness. Licking his lips, he forced himself to be calm. *Normal breaths, old boy. Normal breaths.*

No attack came. After a minute or two, his eyes began to adjust. He could just see inside now. Well enough at least, to compel his legs.

With a last backward glance, Ollie squeezed through the narrow opening. The floor dropped down just beyond the entrance; the ceiling vanished somewhere above. The ruin's interior looked more a cave than any kind of manmade structure. Tumbled brickwork had long since eroded into smooth, featureless walls. He waded through the shadows, picking over a carpet of old, scarred bones. There were no turns, no other passages, and the tight corridor came to an end only eight or nine yards in. *No one's home.* It was clearly a den though. Erörü was close.

A shiver trickled down Ollie's spine. He imagined turning to see the beast behind him, lips curled above pointed

WING

yellow teeth, smoke rising from a blood-matted pelt. Shuddering, he snapped around with his rifle.

Nothing.

Thank Christ, was Ollie's first thought, followed by a half-hearted admonishment for leaving himself open. Then something else occurred to him. As he turned, his foot had grazed an object on the ground. It might have been no more than a rock or a mound of packed earth. He would have failed to notice at all, except when his boot slid across it, there had been a rip. And a clinking metallic spill.

Coins.

Mauser still leveled to the entrance, Ollie dropped to a crouch. He dipped a hand beside him and came up with a dozen or so weighty metal disks. Tilting them into the light, he felt his eyes go wide. They shimmered, almost green in the morning's drifting purple glow. *Gold,* he thought, mystified. *Every coin—the whole sack, probably.* Risking a glance, he found this to indeed be the case. Beneath a brittle strip of leather hanging limp from where he kicked it, a slew of the same heavy coins glittered up at him.

In addition to the one bag, which Ollie had literally stumbled upon, he saw at least six more. Some were amorphously round like the first—more coins, he guessed— others hinted at larger treasures. He even caught sight of a stout wooden locker—an actual treasure chest! Who knew what riches lay waiting in *that*!

Erbörü, you greedy devil. Surprise and excitement cut a toothy line across Ollie's face. *I guess you were every bit the thief Dursun said!* He allowed the coins to slide through his fingers, then scooped another fistful. More wealth in one hand than he would see again in his whole damn life. It was difficult to fathom; so much so, Ollie almost forgot where he was. He nearly forgot what had brought him there to begin with. But as the film of shadows began to recede, as the gold's colour—orange as if by firelight—grew ever more apparent, he allowed his mind to recall.

Orange ... as if...

—*by firelight!*

Ollie took no time to think. Even as he registered the wolf's presence, his Mauser reacted.

Boom!

Confined to the ruin, the weapon's report was enormous; it split open Ollie's skull. A wall of sulphur and smoke appeared between him and the wolf, and a jagged flash bloomed from his target. He had struck just above the creature's shoulder.

Erörü ripped the air with a snarl, but before he could react, Ollie snapped his bolt and fired again. Hot rage scorched the darkness. He loaded another round and took aim. His eyes stung, but his hands were sure. The wolf lurched sideways. He shot him a fourth time. Then he fired again. And again still, emptying his field strip into the beast.

All was silent.

59

The encounter had lasted less than ten seconds.

The man-made cavern shone in the glow of Erbörü's death. Liquid fire painted the floor and spattered the walls around the entrance. Its heat pushed bodily against Ollie's skin.

Before him, his enemy lay unmoving. Ollie lowered his rifle and offered several hurried slaps to where a spray of blood had landed on his clothing and was beginning to smoke.

A rumble rose from the wolf.

He snapped up his rifle. Fumbling in his pocket for another field strip, he slapped five more rounds into the weapon. Erbörü had not shifted from his place on the ground. A long, high whimper extended in his direction. *Alive after all that.*

Alive and on fire.

The stink of burnt fur choked the tunnel.

Ollie felt a stab of sympathy. *Six bullets in him; now he's burning to death from his own blood. I should end it.* He stepped toward the dying animal. As he drew close, he noted what appeared to be a silver bracelet on Erörü's front left leg. *Strange*, he mused, *but why not? After all I've seen tonight, nothing in the world could possibly surprise me.*

He could not have guessed how wrong he was.

Ollie pressed his rifle to the wolf's temple. Erörü's eyes were open, cloudy, yet showing whites all the way around. He fired.

<u>CHAPTER SEVEN</u>
The Prisoner

"OLLIE put his barrel to Erbörü's skull."

Cass leaned in as Gran's voice dropped to just above a whisper. She no longer cared if the story was true, or even possible. She was too swept up, anxious to learn what came next. How did *this* lead to Gran and Ollie meeting at the bridge? Why had Gran never told the story before? Even the miracle of the bracelet—not a half-hour behind her— had dimmed in the shadow of her curiosity.

"The wolf's eyes were open," Gran continued, "glassy, and round with fear. Ollie pressed his finger to the trigger, and … *BOOM!*"

Cass jumped, ejecting a piercing squeak. She slapped a hand over her mouth as if to stuff the embarrassing noise back in. The old woman chortled "Gran!" she half-scolded-half-laughed, clutching at her cardigan. "For Christ's sake, go easy! In your condition you shouldn't— you—you just … well, just focus on getting better, will you?"

"Oh, button it," Gran shot back. "*Getting better.* Last I checked, no one's found a cure for *old*. Besides, *you're* the one chirping like every dog's favorite chew-toy, not me."

"Well, how about taking it easy on me then? Maybe *I'm* in no state to be startled like that." Cass's words were emphatic, but they carried a poorly hidden grin about their edges.

"Okay, dear. I'll try." Gran cleared her throat. Then the muscles in her face tightened. "But that *is* what happened. Such a blast. But not from the gun; it was the wolf. Erbörü *exploded.* It was like something shattered the world. The cave shook. A tornado of fire burst from his chest. Sparks flew everywhere. The roar was like nothing else.

"So, like I said, *boom.*

"The gun fell from your greatest-granddad's hand as he raised his arms against the heat. A noxious reek, like … like … like burning silver, crackled in his lungs. He almost tripped on one of those damn treasure bags, stumbling backward until his shoulders hit the wall at the end of the tunnel. He could only stand there, squinting into that burning, churning inferno, wishing he could burrow through stone to escape it."

The old woman showed a wicked grin. *She's loving this,* Cass thought. It was heartening to see. She smiled back, not daring to interrupt.

"That fire, it was … unlike other fires, unlike the ones Ollie'd chased through the night. Those had been ordinary enough—except where they came from, of course. This was thicker somehow, almost solid. It was hotter too. Much hotter. And it was *changing*. The flames rolled inward, collapsing into themselves, just … just … *becoming*. At the same time, the burning growl in his ears began to-to morph… *Grrrooooouuuzzshh*!" Cass jumped as a dulcet vibration whirred from Gran's chest. "*Zzzsshhhaauughhh*… Soon it almost sounded like a voice.

"Ollie was not looking at a wall of fire. Not a burning wolf, my Cass—Erbörü's carcass was scattered to ashes. The explosion had transformed. Arms, legs, a narrow head piled with thick knots of hair. Long-fingered hands and billowing clothes—baggy trousers and short jacket beneath a fur-lined kaftan.

"Last came the face. Not man nor woman—nor something in-between—it was just …. *else*. With full lips and wide, square teeth. Flaring nostrils clinging to a fantastic beak of a nose. Sharp eyebrows. Fine, strong cheeks. Its eyes were silver-black pools, wild with savage joy!

"The terrible heat faded. Where a scorching storm had raged, now stood a living, breathing being, blinding light dimmed to a faint glow beneath its skin. It was enormous. It towered over Ollie—easily ten feet—and it *screamed*. Like metal being ripped apart. On and on, it bawled, never stopping, not even to breathe.

"What was it?" Cass asked, holding her own breath.

"Ifrit."

She engaged the old woman in a look.

"Do you know what that is, Cassidy?"

Cass knit her brow. Before she had time to consider, Gran supplied the answer. "It's a jinni, dear. The highest, most powerful, most *dangerous* class of jinni."

"Jinni? Like…"

"Like *genie*, yes. We mostly call them *genies* over here, but really, they are *jinn*, powerful fire spirits who share our world. They rarely reveal themselves to mortals, but Greatest-Granddad had stumbled onto one—freed it after long years trapped with the wolf."

"Fire spirit—and that's why he-he *bled* fire?"

Gran nodded. "Infused with the jinni's essence. Ollie would learn this later, when he learned the truth behind Dursun's tale." The old woman cocked her head. "A bit of a detour, but it shouldn't take long if you want to hear."

Indeed, Cass did.

"Well, parts of the farmer's story were true. Erbörü *was* human once, *and* a thief. And he *did* steal from … not a palace—more a wealthy cliffside monastery. And it wasn't some magician who discovered him, but simple guards— *armed* guards with orders to kill any intruders they happened upon. They chased him through the monastery, through a maze of corridors and tunnels, to a dead-end chamber where he barricaded the door. The only way out was a window overlooking a two-hundred-foot drop.

WING

"In his panic, the thief let fall some of his stolen treasures, allowing a thousand-year-old bowl to shatter on the floor. To his amazement, a jinni rose from the broken shards. It spoke to the thief; many years ago, it told him, an ancient enemy had trapped it in clay, then fashioned the dish to contain its power. It had waited so, so, *so* long for someone to break the bowl and free it. Grateful, it promised Erbörü three magical blessings.

"Guards hammered the door, every second a little closer to breaking through, but the thief just stood frozen, goggling up at the jinni. Finally, moments before the wood shattered apart, Erörü awoke to his situation and yelled as loud as his voice could go, 'Give me something to fly from this place!'"

Gran nodded to the item in Cass's hands.

"Bracelet of Ejderha. You saw what it does—*some* of what does. Makes you fly. Also, you won't age while wearing it. Or get sick. A powerful artifact. One of the jinni's most treasured possessions. Without a thought, it gave this item to the thief, who slipped it on his wrist. Suddenly Erörü was flying. Free to escape, he shot out the window to safety. With his life. With his stolen treasures. With an ifrit in his debt."

Cass examined the bracelet. It had not shrunk when she removed it, but remained a perfect fit for her wrist. She resisted the urge to slip it back on. If it stopped aging, why had Gran not worn it herself? *Maybe she wanted a normal life.*

WING

When it comes down to it, who really *wants to live forever?* Somehow that rang false, though. There was something else. *Why does it feel like there's more she isn't telling me?*

This thought set Cass's mind on a path she did not want to see the end of. She hurried to change the subject. "If Erbörü got away, if there was no magician, how did he end up as a wolf?"

Gran raised a chicken-bone finger. "Well, I was about to say, wasn't I?

Cass's mouth snapped shut. She made a motion of buttoning her lips together.

Gran's shoulders rose and fell in a slow harrumph. When Cass held her tongue, the old woman continued. "It wasn't much later, you see, a fortnight or so, when he asked for his second blessing. An … *odd* request. 'Grant me the power to become a wolf,' he demanded. 'Deadlier than any wolf living. Whenever I choose, so I need not run or even fly from those who would capture me, so I can tear them to pieces in my jaws instead!' His words exactly … as Greatest-Granddad related them, that is … as the ifrit had related them to *him*."

She paused theatrically with a furrow in her brow. "Hang on, now … did I say 'odd', Cass? Was that the word I used? 'Odd request'?" Cass bobbed her head. "Oh." Gran mirrored the gesture, biting her lip as if troubled by a sudden thought. "I think I must have meant to say … it was an *idiotic* request. 'Make me a wolf!' Who asks for such a thing? The jinni even *told* Erbörü. But the thief's mind was made up. And do you know what happened?"

A silence passed between them.

"Can you guess?"

Gran seemed to want an answer. Cass shook her head.

"He couldn't turn back!" The old woman's lips tightened around a short, sharp cackle. "Never a wolf was born could become *human*, so neither could he! The first time he transformed, Erbörü was stuck! Ha!"

Gran's breathing came rapid. Cass worried she might be getting too worked up. Before she could try to calm her though, the old woman was already settling back into her pillow. "Foolish man," she sniffed. "Of course, he wasn't the only one to get stuck that day. The jinni had promised *three* blessings and granted only *two*. Until it produced a third—which as a wolf, Erörü could no longer ask for— it was compelled to stay with him. Not to be free until the thief's life had ended.

"Too bad Erörü was wearing that bracelet when he transformed. He wouldn't age. He wouldn't die. Not for centuries. Rather than follow the infernal beast everywhere, walk beside him for years and years … *and years and years* to come, the jinni decided to make a home beneath his skin, fill Erörü like a vessel and weather this latest curse from within. Until someone came at long last to put the wolf out of his misery. Your great-grandfather."

Gran's voice dropped again. She was tiring. She had been talking for hours. Maybe it was time to put an end to this, insist she get some rest. Cass could not bring herself to make the suggestion though. She was snared in her great-grandmother's tale, as caught in the story as the ifrit was within it.

"I guess jinn never learn though," Gran went on. "At least this one didn't. In its excitement to be free, it made the *exact* mistake as the first time.

Standing over Ollie in that dark, narrow space, it raised itself to full height and opened its mouth to speak…"

o   o   o   o

THE figure, not human—too *big* to be human!—but human shaped, appeared to be in shock. Lost within itself, shaking as it seemed to take stock of its own existence, it exhaled a long, panicked mantra. "…free. I'm Free. Free, free; I'm free. I'm free. I'm free…"

After what felt like hours, but could not have been more than a few short minutes, it appeared to calm. In the relapsed darkness, Ollie could make out little beyond its massive silhouette. Its movements—the rapid rise and fall of its back—forceful pulsations between white-knuckled fists and wide, spidering claws—gradually slowed. Finally, the giant stopped. "I am *free*," it breathed one last time, layers of ragged terror and paralyzing joy sliding loose from its voice.

For an eternal minute—time having evaporated from the dimly lit space—they observed one another, statues in a forgotten ruin. Ollie briefly entertained the idea that the being had indeed turned to stone. He even questioned if it had not *always* been stone, if the whole affair—Erbörü, even Tansel and Dursun—were not some mad story he had invented. Surely, none of this was possible, after all. Then the figure moved. Gargantuan hands fell to its sides. Its body rose to full towering height.

"You stand in the presence of an unbound jinni."

The words rumbled through Ollie's bones. Not only could he think of no adequate reply, he was unable to muster a nod or even a blink, to acknowledge he had heard. This seemed to displease the being. When it opened its mouth again, its anger was immense.

"KNEEL MORTAL!"

The command exploded everywhere at once. Stones shook. Ollie cried out as an unseen force thrust him to his knees, causing ribbons of agony to lance up through his legs.

The ruin had grown visible once more beneath the being's—the jinni's—burning silver gaze. Its face was granite and unmistakably human. Yet alien. Celestial. Runnels of icy sweat painted Ollie's face. If he had thought himself frightened before, the vision of power he now craned his neck to look on threatened to swallow his sanity.

He was about to die. He had little doubt.

When the jinni spoke again, however, its voice was calm. "I am Qunae," it said, "First Ifrit of the Sunfall Jinn, Ruler of the Twenty Peaks, Slayer of Serpent-Lord Ejderha, King of Ash and Earthly Flame. Imprisoned once by treachery, and again by unwelcome fate, I am free at long last … thanks to you, human." Though he could feel the blistering press of its attention, Ollie struggled to lift his face to meet it. "You may rise before me."

There was no invisible force this time, nothing impelling his movements, yet as Ollie wobbled to his feet, he did not feel in full control of his body. "Look upon me." His eyes lifted. "By what name do I address my liberator?"

"Oliver. O-O-Oliver Merrill."

"I see you, Oliver Merrill. You have granted me a boon this day, and I am in your debt. Convention dictates I repay you thrice in kind. To this end, I offer you all my magic and abilities. Three blessings you may ask of me. I shall not balk. I shall not leave you until each has been satisfied."

Blood coursing with electricity from the fight, still not recovered from the jinni's shocking arrival—*Qunae*, he told himself; *it calls itself Qunae*—Ollie was slow to register the jinni's words. *Three blessings…* He struggled.

Three…

That sounded like—

70

Three…

Almost like something from a—

Three … wishes?

His heart skipped a beat. *Is that what it just said?* Had Ollie stumbled into some kind of … *fairy-story?* Like Arabian Nights? The wolf had been one thing, but this… Yet here he stood, in a world as real as anything he could smell, taste or hold in his hand, compelled absurdly to ask, *what does one do in such a story? What does one ask for?*

Three wishes…

Then a fog seemed to lift from his eyes.

Through his travels, Ollie had come to recognize that there was something missing in his life. Something had *always* been missing. He had been so sure he would find it in Turkey, eventually, if he searched long enough. At the farm, he almost believed he had. Now with a world of possibilities at his fingertips, he saw he had been mistaken. It was not his life here that had so drawn him to Dursun and Tansel; he was not after some pastoral dream of tranquility. He wanted what he saw when he looked at them. He wanted what they had in each other.

Despite the jinni's crushing stare, Ollie could not help but laugh. *How God damn ordinary,* he marvelled. His affliction—the search that had drawn him across this country—would have ended the same had he simply gone home after the war. Ollie, as it turned out, wanted nothing more than any young man in any city, village or farm across the planet.

Destiny. Leave it to me to find the most uncommon, extraordinary, and utterly ridiculous path to achieving it!

The jinni continued to observe him.

Straightening his back, Ollie met Qunae's glowing onyx eyes. "I wish to find my one true love," he said, grinning at the preposterousness of his words. "A girl I'll never want to be apart from, one with whom I'll want to spend the rest of my life."

The ifrit did not laugh, as Ollie himself had. It merely inclined its head.

"This," it said slowly, "is within my power."

CHAPTER EIGHT
Deep Rains

"THIS is within my power."

The moment passed. Ollie swallowed. His brain still buzzed with shock. The whole world seemed to vibrate. *Wait, what did I just ask for?* It was difficult to think. Seconds-old memories felt slippery in his mind. *Love. Yes, of course. To meet my true love.* He looked about the ruin. The girl of his dreams would not simply step from the shadows and introduce herself ... would she?

Qunae noted his uncertainty. "No, Oliver Merrill," it rumbled. "You will not find her in this place. I have set her on your path. As you continue your journey, she will reveal herself."

Ollie straightened and tried to focus. He retrieved his rifle from the remains-strewn floor where he had dropped it. This was it then, an end to his travels. At last, he had found what he was searching for. Destiny lay naked before, and he was eager to meet it.

That would also mean leaving the farm...

Tansel and Dursun were beside themselves when Ollie returned. Neither had slept. They were so relieved to see him, they scarcely seemed to care what fate had befallen the wolf. He related the encounter anyway—omitting a few key details.

Upon learning they had escaped Erbörü's unwelcome attention, Tansel insisted they celebrate with a feast. Ollie declined. He wished to ride for a while, he said; he needed to think. In truth, he spent the day hauling treasure back from Erbörü's den. It was his to claim, he figured, as the original owners had long since turned to dust.

The next morning, he set out.

Dursun and Tansel were in the yard when Ollie emerged from the barn for the last time. He had said nothing of his intentions to go—goodbyes were messy—but somehow, they knew. Tansel pushed a pack into his arms. She had stuffed it with hard breads, cheeses, vegetables, and spicy salted goat—enough food to last him for days. Dursun presented him with a pair of sturdy leather suspenders; a perfect fit. They embraced him as a son, kissed him on the lips, and told him he would always have a place at their table.

Ollie hugged and kissed them back, knowing he would never return to the farm; he would see neither again in life. Blinking back tears—dammit, goodbyes *were* messy!—he turned and headed away, up the narrow dirt track. He made no mention of the treasure, which he had left in the barn

WING

where one of them was sure to find it. Erbörü's wealth was theirs. No two people better deserved it. For himself, he kept only the bracelet.

And the jinni's debt.

Qunae appeared at Ollie's side as the farm vanished behind him. The ifrit had taken human shape. Exactly what that shape was, was difficult to say. Half the time it looked like a middle-aged man, short, thin and nondescript; the other half, it was a tall, plain, equally forgettable young woman. As far as Ollie could tell, it never actually transformed from one into the other; it just suddenly *was*. He was not even certain, at times, which of the jinni's veils he was looking at, or if there was in fact difference between them. "A deception of the mind," Qunae explained. "You see what you are least likely to remember. Eyes slide past me as if I do not exist. Travellers will see me without noticing, notice without recalling." As the days passed, even to Ollie's knowing gaze, this certainly seemed to be the case.

They made for the last town Ollie had come through before reaching the farm. It began to rain the very morning they set out, continuing through the rest of their journey. Each day they watched the river rise a little higher.

"It'll be spilling banks by the time we arrive," Ollie said, expecting no replay from the ifrit. Qunae was proving a somewhat laconic travel companion. On that first morning, after recounting how it came to live in Erörü's skin,

75

inexorably bound by its own fateful promise, it had grown quiet, showing little regard for casual conversation. Still, Ollie could not help trying. "Crossing that bridge of theirs may prove a bit tricky, I think."

No reply.

Ollie sighed.

They were headed for Uğursuz Köprü, a town whose name meant … *Unfit Bridge? Broken Bridge, maybe? Something about a bridge.* Ollie could not recall what *Uğursuz* translated to, though he suspected it was bad. And from what he remembered, *bad* was a near-perfect description.

Progress slowed as rain quickly transformed their road into a channel of covetous mud. Tansel's provisions gave out early on the fifth day, and through the last leg of their journey Ollie was compelled to forage. He shot a good-sized rabbit, only to realize he had no way to cook the damned thing. Beneath these bawling skies, he could find no scrap of wood, bark or grass dry enough to carry a flame. Some hours later, he spotted an entourage of jackals on the trail behind him. They showed no signs of aggression, keeping mostly out of sight, but were unnervingly persistent. They dogged Ollie for hours before he gave in and threw his kill into the bushes, sending a flush of fur and wild, hungry yips chasing after it. *At least someone gets to eat tonight*, he told himself with a gloomy twist of the mouth. He certainly wanted none of the sharp-toothed little

WING

bastards sniffing around his camp, or rooting through his pack while he slept.

The next morning, they reached the town.

The bridge was as bad as Ollie remembered. It consisted of three long ropes connected by a number of smaller support lines. *Too small a number if you ask me*, he might have complained if he thought Qunae cared to listen. The main ropes were secured on either bank to a set of heavy wooden pylons, and staked down with iron spikes. There were no planks to step on, only a single line on the bottom and one for each hand. As Ollie recalled, this made for rather precarious footing—and that had been in the dry season! As it stood, the bottom rope actually dropped into the river's current, pulling the whole structure into a sickening twist.

Well this couldn't be much worse, he observed, eyes pinching onto the lines stretched before him. *Crossing here looks like … suicide.* He seemed to recall there was another bridge, somewhat out of the way but considerably safer than what he was looking at. If only he could remember which direction it had been in.

As Ollie stood pondering, rain and exhaustion blurring his vision, a gradual shock settled over him. *What the hell?* Without quite realizing, he had been staring at a person *already* on the bridge, a small figure in a storm-coloured coat, clinging to the pitching ropes. This brave soul had made it past the submerged stretch in the middle, and was nearly two-thirds the way to the other bank.

Ollie's stomach roiled.

Shuffling closer, he followed the stranger's progress. *If that madman can make it*, he assured himself silently, not entirely certain how well he believed, *so can I.* This thought, however, was no more than a sheen of oil atop the much deeper, much darker pool of awareness. Beneath it, his mind offered different words. *That fool's going to die*, it whispered. For something else lay hidden in the scene before him, something he could not quite put his finger on. Something about it looked … *wrong.*

Then Ollie realized.

He had failed to notice, as it was still well upstream. Once he saw though, he could not look away. An old-growth cedar, ripped from its place on the bank, had fallen into the river. Now a passenger, it rose steadily toward the bridge.

"Hey!" Ollie shouted. "Hello! Hey, look! He-e-y-y-y!" The figure did not turn. "Look out! Get off the bridge!" No good. The storm devoured his warnings before any trace could reach the imperilled traveller. Ollie eyed the approaching tree, the distance he would have to cross to get to the stranger. How fast would he have to go? How fast *could* he go?

He would realize some time later, it never occurred to him to ask for Qunae's help. They had spoken so little on the journey, he had no doubt forgotten the jinni's presence. *Not to mention the stress of the situation*, he liked to add any time the memory resurfaced. *Not quite panic, but something close.* He did his best to remember it this way … because the alternative was unthinkable. Perhaps, asking the jinni *had* occurred to him. Perhaps, he was simply too selfish to waste one of his precious wishes on another person. He hated to think this of himself, and never truly accepted it, but … perhaps.

Neither did it occur to Ollie to use the bracelet however, to fly across and pluck the stranger from the bridge. So maybe, in that strained moment, it *was* blind instinct that drove him forward. Or perhaps, even a different thought propelled him on that miserable Turkish morning. A stupefying, gut-wrenching thought, beside which no other could exist.

I have to save her!

The words materialized in Ollie's mind with such force, he quite nearly shouted them. Without knowing how—or even realizing he knew—he suddenly grasped the figure's identity. This was the person he was searching for. He was seeing for the first time, the love of his life, the girl he would adore until the day he died. And he would be damned if he let her drown the moment he laid eyes on her.

"No," Ollie growled, sliding a foot onto the jerking line, catching the hand ropes in white-knuckled fists.

WING

"Hang on!" he cried into the wind, knowing she was still too far to hear. "I'm coming!"

Without another thought, he stepped onto the bridge to save the woman he loved. To claim the destiny that awaited him.

<u>CHAPTER NINE</u>
The Englishman

"BUT he *didn't* save you," Cass grinned. "You saved *him.*"

They had finally come back to the beginning, yet Cass wondered what more could be left. Gran and Ollie had met now; was that not the story? Though, surely the genie had a greater part to play. And the two remaining wishes. Or were these mere footnotes in their romantic epic?

No, she thought. *No, there is more. Gran's building to something; I can tell.* Something was coming.

Even as Cass considered what was being said, her mind tumbled back, recalling words that had shocked her the first-time round. "Wait, Gran ... what you said before ... you said you'd wished Greatest-Granddad *drowned.*"

Gran blinked. She reached for her water and took a long, careful sip. Unspoken words scored the sterile air between them. *I did say that, yes.* Cass could almost hear the woman's voice. *And I'll even tell you what I meant, if you can resist piping in every few seconds.*

81

She cleared her throat and mumbled an apology.

Gran smacked her lips and set down her cup. "Don't give it another thought, dear."

The story resumed.

"The young woman—little older than a girl, really—"

"Ayla." Cass could not recall the last time she had heard someone use Gran's given name. She was fairly certain this was the first time *she* had said it aloud. She bit down on her lip, realizing she was interrupting again.

"Was that what she was called?" Gran's mouth twitched coyly. "Okay then, Ayla. Yes, *Ayla* pulled Ollie from the river when the tree threatened to sweep him away. And yes, when she saw the way he looked at her, the hunger in his eyes, the *certainty*—even half-drowned as he was—she wondered if it had not been a mistake to do so.

"But it was too late; she had saved him. Like it or not, she was responsible. She brought him to her home to rest the night, as a guest of her family. He was still a stranger, mind you, and as far as she knew, he always would be.

"When she left with her brother Berat the next morning, Ayla thought she would never see the Englishman again. This, as I guess you know, would not be the case…"

o   o   o   o

82

"LOOK! Look at these. Here! *Worms*. Look—look! Worms … worms … *more* worms! From what Satan-blighted grove did you find these terrible figs?"

The man pushing his fists into Berat's gawping face smelled of old food and unwashed human crevices. Though he could not have been much older than Ayla herself—twenty-one at the most—wrapped in layers of wretchedness as he was, he looked nearly middle-aged.

Berat shuffled back. Whether to escape the piquant odour, gain some distance from the infested fruit, or simply in retreat of the man's aggressive stance, Ayla could not say. "I-I'm sorry," the boy managed. "I don't know where—or how—oh… We've never had this problem before."

"Worms!" the man sang again, tearing another fig to reveal a tiny squirming shape.

"I-I—"

"Look at them! I bought these just yesterday, and you give me this rot? I demand the money I paid!" Her brother's eyes darted from the outthrust hands, bare inches from his face, to the slotted strongbox at the back of their stall. "What are you waiting for, boy? Give me my money!"

Appearing from nowhere, the enraged man had startled them both. But while Ayla, familiar with such street theatrics, was quick to recover, Berat remained flustered. The boy reacted with his nerves, she knew, never his head. He

WING

was going to panic and give the man what he demanded, if only to escape the situation.

Shouldering her brother aside, Ayla slapped a hand over one the hustler's. She held firm as he immediately tried to pull away. "Please, sir, let me see." She kept her voice cool and polite. A single glance was enough. "These aren't ours." Ayla squeezed one of the too-hard bulbs and watched it crunch between her forefinger and thumb. "Everyone knows *ours* are always ripe. Also, *these*..." flicking through the man's figs until she found what she was looking for, "...these have been slit open so *you* could slip the worms in yourself!" Casting his hand away, she tore one of his figs to reveal the unwelcome occupant within. "Worms," she said, mocking his feigned outrage. "*Your* worms."

The con man had already begun to back away. His head swivelled dramatically, eyes darting about. How many in the market had heard the exchange? *Plenty,* Ayla thought. *He* had made no effort to temper his voice. Neither had she.

"Thief!" Berat howled from behind her. "Hustler! Liar! Thief!" Before Ayla could stop him, the boy was flying forward, waving a three-foot cane he had cut from the tree behind their house—his *bandit stick*, as he liked to call it.

"Berat!" she snapped, failing to catch him as he sprinted past. "Berat, come back!" Too late. Quick as he arrived, the scammer vanished into an alleyway, her brother in pursuit. "*Berat!*"

Ayla sighed.

Cowing her brother was the easiest thing in the world. When it came to his honour however, he was like a dog with a bone. *He'll dive head first into a lion's den if I say the lion insulted him*, she mused glumly. *And I bet* this *mangy lion has more dens than a whole colony of rabbits.*

Berat would not be back soon.

This prediction proved true. The afternoon drained by without sight or sign of her brother. The swindler had lost him at once, Ayla suspected, leaving the boy to spend hours poking his head into alleys and dark corners, hoping to stumble back upon him. "*Bring your brother*," she burbled in an exaggerated cadence of her mother's voice. "*He can help drum up sales in the market.*" There was little to do about it now, though. Only keep selling her figs. And nurse the sisterly annoyance boiling in her belly.

And this was just what Ayla did. She stood. She sold. She stewed. Even as orange light glazed the plaza's atmosphere and shadows grew longer around her, she continued to grind her teeth, startling neighboring vendors with occasional un-ladylike growls. What good were brothers, anyway? A girl was certainly better off without.

Then another face materialized at her stall, vanishing all thoughts of her brother.

"Good afternoon." Bright-eyed and pale, Oliver Merrill directed a confident English smile in her direction.

"Oh!" Ayla started at his sudden appearance. "Oh, it's you—ah—I mean … *hello*. Peace be upon you. You're feeling better, I'm happy to see."

"Indeed." The Englishman stepped a little closer. "Thanks to you, I should say. And to your parents, of course. They were kind to care for me overnight."

"It was nothing," she assured him.

Oliver Merrill shook his head.

And he continued to stand there. Watching her.

"Well … um…" Ayla suspected she ought to say more, but words eluded her. This man made her uncomfortable. His manner was pleasant enough, but there was something in the way he regarded her which she found to be off-putting. "Would you like a fig?" she asked at last, unable to think of anything better. He accepted the offering and held it in front of him without taking a bite. "And … and … and I hope, God willing, your business in town proves felicitous." She clenched her lips in a practiced vendor's beam.

Oliver Merrill did not move. "Your father said I'd find you here." His voice was still hoarse from the river.

Ayla nodded again but said nothing.

"Yes," he coughed, "well … I just wanted to come thank you once more, in person." He pocketed the fig and pushed out his hand.

The motion recalled Ayla to the reeking hustler with his worms. Though she gripped her skirt to dry her palm, she did not shake. "I am pleased to see you again," she replied instead, doing her best to sound amiable.

His smile faltered. He lowered his arm. "Your parents invited me to lunch with your family tomorrow."

"Lunch? Tomorrow?" Ayla fumbled. They invited him back? Why? "I…"

"I'll be glad for the chance to speak with you some more."

"Yes, that will be very … um … pleasant."

"I hope I'll have thought of a way to thank you properly by then. Maybe we—"

Whatever Oliver Merrill was going to suggest was cut short as a familiar voice rent the air. "Away! Away, foreign monster! Leave my sister!"

The Englishman dodged back, narrowly escaping a downward slice from her baby brother's bandit stick. "Whoa!" he expelled in a friendly bark. "Well met, little man!"

"Berat!" Ayla scolded. "Berat, stop it with that idiot stick! Get in here. Where in Creation have you been?" Glad for an excuse to turn from the Englishman, she focused on her brother. "Don't you know you left me here to work all by myself? Don't you know you're supposed to be *helping*? Not chasing poor wretches and foreigners all through the streets? Put that thing away! Put it down now!"

When she was certain Oliver Merrill had moved off, Ayla straightened and took a step back from her brother. The boy's cheeks shone crimson and wet. "I'm sorry, Sister—" he began.

"Never mind." She squeezed Berat's shoulder and rubbed his back. "Forget what I said. You did well. God be good, you did right. Except in leaving me to work by myself. That *was* bad."

"Yes, Sister." Berat wiped a sleeve across his face. "I won't do it again, God willing. I promise."

"Good," Ayla mumbled absently. "Please remember next time."

Her mind had already drifted past her brother and his tears, though. Oliver Merrill would be returning to the house. And she had a good idea what he hoped to get from the engagement.

Yes, Ayla thought, grimly. *Engagement. That really is the word, I think.*

The Englishman was going to be trouble.

CHAPTER TEN
Puppet Love

AYLA managed to escape the objectionable lunch. Though it took her a couple tries. First, she claimed she could not spare the time, that hosting the foreigner would interfere with her daily excursions—which were important, as they helped support the family. Her father dismissed this at once, however. "You need only return from the groves an hour early," he had said. "Afterward, you should have no problem making it to the plaza for the usual time."

He was right, of course, and Ayla was compelled to come up with something a little more drastic. Claiming to feel a touch strange that night after prayer, she pretended the next morning to be struck by a sudden illness. She was too sick to gather figs, she said, too sick to get out of bed. Certainly, too sick for company.

"The Englishman wants to thank you properly," her father had insisted. "It's unthinkable you should miss it." It would be far worse, she argued, to receive the foreigner, hacking fluids and half delirious with fever. She punctuated this with an extended fit of coughing, allowing her father no opportunity to reply. And no choice but to leave her be. In the end, he relented. What else could he do?

Ayla's mother seemed to suspect.

Even as she fed Ayla yogurt with garlic, and mint tea to settle her stomach, something in her voice suggested she knew. "He's very handsome," she murmured, kneeling beside the bed. "And charming. Your father's quite enamoured, I think." Ayla choked on the hot liquid. "Of course," the older woman added, taking her cup, "my husband *does* love his strays. And God knows, he can't always see when one shouldn't be let in the house. The young man is English, after all. And Christian. And a man." Ayla smiled at this. "Depending what the boy says today—what he *asks*—we may see your father's affections run dry for him."

Ayla took comfort in her mother's words.

Better still, they proved true.

Oliver Merrill came late in the morning and left close to an hour later. Muffled voices carried through the walls, sounding warm and pleasant, but when her father appeared afterward, his face was cold steel. He clutched a rifle in his hand, holding it at arm's length as he might a venomous snake.

"He gave me this," he said, offering no explanation of why, or what the two of them had discussed.

WING

Ayla was prepared to make a guess though. *He's asked Father's permission to court me.* It was exactly as she had feared.

Her father, on the other hand, looked stunned, and more than a little appalled. In some ways, he was as naïve as Berat. At least he recognized the gift for what it was. A bribe. For which *she* was the desired payment. "You are not to seek that man's company or accept or his affections," was all he said to her. Still feigning sick, Ayla nodded her compliance.

And so, the matter was concluded.

Or at least … so she thought.

o   o   o   o

IT was three days later when she saw Oliver Merrill again. The rains had stopped the day she rescued the Englishman, but the air remained damp and cool. The sun rose dawnless behind a faceless sheet of clouds and was full up by the time she reached the southern bridge. Plenty of light to make out the figure standing before it.

"Good morning, sweet Ayla," Oliver Merrill sang to her as she approached. Ayla did not call back. He waited, watching her slow march toward him.

She sighed.

She could not simply walk past without acknowledging him. Even to a foreigner, she could not bring herself to be so rude. Instead, she halted a good fifteen feet from where he stood.

"Peace be upon you, Oliver Merrill," she offered quietly. She did not raise her eyes above his collar, focussing rather on a cloth pack held in his fist. Mild curiosity—layered with traces of suspicion—trickled through her mind at the sight. But Ayla would not ask about it. *If I refuse to engage, he must see there's no hope of catching my eye.*

"Hectic life you lead," he said.

"Yes, I am very busy."

Oliver Merrill attempted a chuckle. It sounded closer to an anxious sneeze. "I've noticed. I've been—I mean … I've seen you about town, making these trips early each morning, then to the market to sell what you collect."

Watching me. The thought made Ayla's spine itch. "Yes, it's a lot of work."

For a moment, they stood in silence. The Englishman, it seemed, could think of nothing more to say. She allowed herself a granule of hope. *Maybe he'll go now.* Then she saw the rifle slung over his shoulder, the same rifle he had given her father. How did he have it again? No matter. She would not ask.

This has gone on long enough, Ayla judged. Prematurely perhaps, but she was eager move on. *It won't be rude if I start walking now. Just nod politely and be on my way.*

As she lifted her foot, however, Oliver Merrill found his voice. "I'm afraid I'm not made for such dancing about," he admitted, scraping the earth with the edge of his boot. "I'm more like to leap in blind—not worry the drop till I've landed. As you well saw on the river, I guess. That usually works for me—and it did then too, because … because it led me to you."

Ayla's eyes widened. Her mind raced as he continued to speak. She needed to extract herself from this situation before things started to compound.

"So, let me just say it then, clear and simple: I believe we are meant for each other. I believe we were *supposed* to meet on that bridge, that we're supposed to be together. The moment I saw your face, I thought—I thought—I…" Though his mouth kept moving, no more sounds escaped.

Oliver Merrill glanced over his shoulder. Ayla followed his gaze, and for the first time, noticed a waif of a man in earth-coloured robes standing on the bridge. *How did I not see him before?* She wondered with a start. For his part, the Englishman seemed to find comfort in the sight of his companion. Turning back toward her, he spoke the word she had been dreading since laying eyes on him. "The moment I saw you, I knew it was *love*."

Ayla resisted the urge to take a quick pace back.

"Here." He held the bag toward her. "I know how long it takes you to pick all those figs each day. I thought I might help. I thought, if I gave you a little extra time, you might agree to join me for a stroll along the river."

Ayla made no move for the pack. "That rifle," she said, wholly ignoring his offer. "Did you not present that as a gift to my father?"

Oliver Merrill touched the weapon's strap. "He didn't mention, then? That I called on you, day before last, and he … gave it back to me? He insisted I take it. I think he's against us being together."

"My father respects my wishes." Ayla finally lifted her gaze to meet Oliver Merrill's. He was chewing the inside of his mouth, and a shadow had appeared above the bridge of his nose. This was going differently than he had expected.

"Look," he said, "I don't care what your father says, or your mother, or-or your *little brother*; I know we're meant for each other! You must see it! You must!" He threw another glance to his companion on the bridge. This caused Ayla to start again; she had forgotten the young woman was there. *Wait … wasn't there a man there before? No, of course not.* She dismissed the thought and forgot she had ever had it.

Her eyes returned to Oliver Merrill. Wetting her lips, she considered her words carefully. "You say we are meant to be together; how can you know this? How can *you* speak to the song in *my* heart? How, when my words fall deaf to your ears? Why, if fate twines us as you claim, is it only *you* who knows this? And if I am *your* destiny, how is it I know, with unshakable certainty, that you are *not* mine?" She

WING

stepped toward him, closing the gap. "You say you love me; what doom would you have me meet to satisfy your love?"

"I *do* love you," Oliver Merrill answered, somehow missing everything she had said.

Ayla swallowed her frustration. "I thank you for your love."

He seemed to choke a little. "I'll take you away from here, bring you back to England and——"

Ayla screamed. Lunging, she seized the sack of figs and swung toward the bridge. A storm of fruit filled the air, raining down in a cascade of wet *twop*s. "You will take me *nowhere*! Who are you, you-you, *foreign parasite*? Who are you that I should leave my *home*, my *family*, just because you ask? God saw fit to let me save your life when I should have *let that tree take you!* Yet instead of showing gratitude, instead of *humility*, you come demanding *my life* too?!"

Blood hammered at the back Ayla's skull. Each breath was a labour to contain. She drew closer to the Englishman, no idea what she was about to do. She wanted to push him in the river. She wanted to kick him; she had never felt anger like this. So it was no small surprise when she watched herself reach out calmly and strip him of his rifle. Even more shocking, when she opened her mouth, the voice that came out sounded both mild and reasoned. "You offered this to my father as a gift," she said. "I will see that it finds him again." Ayla did not know how to carry

95

the weapon—it was the first time she had held one—and she found herself gripping it like Berat with his bandit stick. She ignored how foolish this no doubt made her look. "Now, as for your figs, your stroll along the river, and your promise to *take me from my home*, you may hold them for the next girl, and God willing, be on your way. May He see you safely on your journey."

With a sniff, Ayla strode past this solider who saw fit to claim her. She resolved not to turn back, not even to check if he was following. She would give him no such satisfaction. Eyes forward, she stepped through the minefield of spilled figs—*Fool doesn't even know to leave the unripened ones*—crunching a too-hard bulb beneath her foot.

She crossed the bridge, passing the peculiar little man. It troubled her that, yet again, his presence had slipped her mind. *And hadn't he been… No, it doesn't matter.* She continued her march away, leaving the presumptuous Englishman forever behind her.

o   o   o   o

DRAWN between enchantment and despair, Ollie watched until the road turned west, vanishing Ayla from sight. "She hates me," he said to the ifrit, who continued to observe him from the bridge. "I've known nothing like what I feel for her—what I've felt since the moment I saw her face—but … she'll have nothing of it."

WING

Qunae just nodded.

Ollie suppressed a growl. "She's supposed to be the love of my life. She's *supposed* to be my dream girl!"

"You will love her until the day you die," the jinni intoned quietly.

"I don't understand."

"Bestowing blessings on mortals is no common pursuit among ifrit, Oliver Merrill. We know little of your kind, and we do not presume. I remain grateful to you, and would cause you no deliberate harm, but I cannot interpret your desires beyond the words you use to speak them. Erbörü asked for the power to become a wolf, so I granted it. *You* asked to meet a woman you will adore all your life. Now you have."

"But she doesn't love me!" This drew a flat stare from the jinni. Ollie grunted as if struck. "Because..." he muttered, tumbling the immortal's words in his head, "...because I didn't ask for someone who *would*, only someone *I* would love." His eyes drifted back to the road. To the spot where he had last seen her. *She'll never want me.* The thought pulled icy rills into his chest; his whole ribcage seemed to clench. *She'll never—she'll* never *choose to be with me.*

"But then, of course," Qunae's voice sliced through Ollie's bitter reverie, "two blessings remain. I could *make* her love you."

"No," Ollie answered at once. "That would be monstrous."

WING

"Monstrous? To deny her what you seek for yourself? When I could craft in her such feelings as she would wish never to be apart? As she would never know she had felt anything different?"

Ollie hesitated. Could he make such a wish?

No.

No. He would not strip Ayla of her will. He would not force unwanted feelings on her, no matter how happy he knew he could make her. Such a thing would be … evil.

He was about to say as much when the ifrit—who had perhaps read his thoughts—offered another solution. "Or I could make a replica. Not a person, not alive—creating life is beyond me—but something that *looks* like her, speaks with the same voice. It would mimic her personality. Her fire. Only *it* will not scorn you. It will accept your affections and return them in kind."

Ollie chomped down on the inside of his mouth, grinding his cheek between molars. What was Qunae saying? *Another* Ayla?

"Your love for it—for *her*—will be no different than what you feel for the other."

The same woman, only … it will love me? "Would it be real?"

"Real enough to stay with you, to share your life as you grow old. She could even give you children." Ollie swallowed. He wanted to look away, but the mercury blaze in Qunae's eyes refused to release him. "I cannot *create* life, but I can forge in her the ability to brew offspring from

98

your seed alone. Living, *human* children. Your life with her will be just as it could have been with the first."

Ollie needed a moment. He crouched to scoop up a clump of damp earth—it was the only way he could think to break the jinni's gaze. His heart exacted a vengeance against the front wall of his chest; breaths came in short trembling bursts. *It would be an illusion. Not a woman at all.* He ground the cold dirt between his fingers. Would that be enough? Could it? What if it had to be? What if that was all that was left for him? He would suffer her absence his whole life; his own words had ensured this. Did he really think he could handle that?

"I wish…" he began. His voice caught in his throat. Was this really what he wanted?

Ayla would live on without him. One day she would meet someone she could love, and *they* would build a life together. Ollie had his own happiness to consider. And why not? He was as entitled to it as anyone. *Say the words, you coward!*

"I wish for a double of Ayla." He stood, clapping the soil from his palms. "One to return my love, just as you say. One that will join me in life's adventures. Someone to have a family with, to grow old with. Someone to love … who will make me feel loved."

Qunae stroked its chin. "This is within my power."

No sooner had it spoken than a figure stepped from behind its back.

WING

Ollie's gaze touched the jinni's creation, and gasp slipped from his lips. *Good Heavens! My God, it looks just like her.* He could discern no difference, whatsoever, between the figure in front of him and the one whose scorn he had so recently swallowed.

The replica eyed Ollie modestly, almost nervously. "So," it said in Turkish, in a voice sounding of music, a voice already imprinted to his soul. "How about that walk?"

Ollie could not speak. He stood breathless.

Perfect. It was utterly perfect. A perfect … simulation.

CHAPTER ELEVEN
Behind Her Eyes

THE initial shock soon faded, and a forest of doubts rose in Ollie. *Could this still be love? This? For something that was ... created for me?* Surely, love needed to be shared; surely, it required some kind of connection between people—*real* people. No matter how the thing before him resembled Ayla, however perfect a replica, he would always be alone in its company. The feelings between them, they were his only, merely reflected back in the eyes of an automaton. How could *that* be love?

God, it was beautiful though.

Ollie had trouble facing it. He tried—he *truly* did—but he could not free himself from the confines of his head. "How about that walk?" it had asked. All he could think was, *this thing wasn't here when I invited Ayla to walk with me—Ayla who left. It didn't even exist yet; how can it remember?* Knowing this as he did, Ollie could not pretend he was looking at the same woman. No matter if his eyes—or even his heart—avowed it.

They did not stroll along the river that day.

Setting out from Uğursuz Köprü, he could not bring himself to walk beside the jinni's creation, or sit with it when they made camp, even as it tried to engage with him. "Give me time," he begged on their second night, though he could imagine no length of time that would unknot his doubts. The creation seemed to understand.

Which was more than Ollie could say.

"How can it be her?" he asked, some days later as the replica made its ablutions. "Ayla *hated* me. How could this be the same girl, but love me instead?"

Qunae, appearing in its guise of a young woman, looked thoughtful for a moment. "She does not love you, Oliver Merrill," it said. "She does not *love*. Or think. Or feel. She is a vacillating shell of fire and tempered aether, which I have sculpted into a pleasing shape for you. She only acts as the original would if *she* had loved you. Under different circumstances, she could have."

Bitter words.

"Humans feel so much and understand so little," the ifrit observed. "As I have said before, I am not well versed in your kind, but I know this: what you call love is like a sickness. Feed it the right conditions, it can catch hold of anyone. Had Ayla witnessed less of her people's blood spilled by your own—had *you* approached her with the barest shade of delicacy—she may have realized emotions to match your own."

Ollie deflated. Qunae's words carried all the confirma-tion he needed. *Vacillating shell... Does not love or think or feel...* It had offered answer to the question he had deliber-ately *not* asked. Because he was already sure what that an-swer would be. Because he could not bear to hear it. Ayla—this Ayla—*his Ayla*—would never be more than an empty mask, a puppet controlled by the jinni.

You knew this though, he reminded himself. *From the begin-ning.* Ollie supposed he had allowed himself to hope that somehow, in some small way, it could be different. Even this hope was gone now.

There were no more questions after that.

At length, their strange party found its way to Istanbul. Ollie bullied, bartered, and begged them spots on a cargo ship, in exchange for which he and Ayla—the thing calling itself Ayla—were compelled to work, him in the engine room and her ... *it* in the galley. No such requirement for Qunae. The jinni simply walked aboard, earning neither comment nor look from anyone in the crew.

Ollie saw little of Ayla through the first leg of their voy-age. The boatswain had assigned them a tiny corner in the deepest hold, and though for the next forty-one days this was to be their home, he remained quiet a stranger to the place. Rising early each morning, he spent his days trim-ming coal. The work was grueling, yet when Ollie's shift ended in the evenings, he rarely found his way back before midnight. Rather than face the discord of emotions

WING

awaiting him below, he delayed his rest, wandering the ship, dog-tired, until he could be sure his *fiancé* was asleep.

What am I going to do? he would ask himself through these long, dismal hours, staring across the fading blue plain. *Where do I go from here?* As far as he figured, there was but one avenue of escape. Qunae still owed him a blessing. He just had to demand it. *Undo the other wishes. Get rid of her. Of it. Scrub this love from my heart.* He only needed to ask, and the ordeal would be over.

But then, of course … it would be over. No more magic. No more miracles. No love. Ollie would return with nothing.

Fine then. I can live with that. And he supposed he probably could. That was not even the problem though. The thought of having squandered his wishes, having wasted the miraculous fortune he had uncovered in Turkey, was a pebble beneath the cloud-piercing mountain of his true concern: could he really do that? It felt like he would be killing her, regardless of what Qunae said. No less murder than if he snapped her neck and dropped her body over the side.

It was stupid. She was counterfeit; he *knew* this. How could just the idea of erasing her bother him as it did? *She's alive, or she* isn't, *God damn it. You can't believe both at once!* No matter how he crushed this thought against his skull, however, it refused to take hold.

The storm of doubts finally broke on the thirteenth day of their voyage.

The sun had extinguished itself in the ocean's distant cradle; its flames still burned on the horizon, casting wave after scarlet wave across a platinum-sapphire sky. He came upon her suddenly, staring over the water as he so often did. It was the first time since they boarded that Ollie had seen her abovedeck. He almost walked away. He almost turned on his heels and ran. But his joints resisted the impulse; he was so tired, physically, emotionally, spiritually. *What's the point? Avoiding her gets you nowhere. Like it or not, she's in this with you.* And for the first time since Ayla appeared, Ollie approached her to share a moment.

Though she did not turn, there was no question she saw him pressed to the railing beside her. "God knows, I'm trying to be patient." Her voice was quiet and thick with emotion.

Ollie dug a hand into his breast pocket and came away with a cigarette. His last. He had been saving it for days. He lit it and inhaled gratefully, then he held it out it to Ayla. She shook her head. He took another drag, considered it for a second, then flicked it away, vanishing it into the void.

"I don't exactly understand it," she said. "I know it's hard for you too. I thought, if I gave you time … if I gave you the space you needed … but it's not getting better, is it? I just couldn't take another minute hiding away in that hold. I couldn't—I just … I—" Quavering words seemed to catch in her throat.

Despite himself, Ollie rested a hand on her shoulder and offered a light squeeze. "Please don't cry." Ayla turned to face him. Tears glazed her eyes, but her furrowed visage showed no hint of anguish.

"I'm not *crying*, you oaf!" She knocked his arm away then struck him in the soft spot between shoulder and chest. Ollie grunted at the painful jolt. "I'm *not* crying! I'm telling you, you get no more time! I'm done hiding for your benefit!" She hit him again—harder—in the same spot, then once more—harder still—in the sternum. Ollie stumbled back against the assault. "I *know* you love me every bit as much as I love you." She punctuated the words *love* with a punch in the stomach, then a slap to his face.

"I'm sorry," Ollie blurted automatically. "I-I—" Whatever he was going to say was cut short by another blow.

"Enough! If *you* want to hide, go right ahead." She leaned into a shove, then immediately closed the distance to strike him several more times. "But God knows, you shouldn't! You should *want* to be with me! You should want to talk to me—want to *hold* me! You love me, you foreign idiot!"

"I-I—" Ollie struggled to justify himself. It took all his concentration just to stave off her attacks. There was no time to think; the words tumbled from his mouth independent of any thought. "I *do* love you. I—"

She hit him again.

"Then stop being difficult!" Ayla grabbed him by the collar and shook. Ollie opened his mouth to… *protest?* … *apologize?* He could only venture a guess.

He would never find out.

Before he could utter another word, Ayla lunged. Her lips found his; their mouths pressed together. Ollie jumped at the burst of energy passing through him, but she refused to let him go. She breathed him in … devoured him … drowned him, forcefully, angrily, hungrily. Even as he considered what to do, he found he was already kissing her back. He drew her toward him, inhaling her—all of her— the warmth of her breath, her saliva mixing with his, her hands' urgent clutch and the softness of her skin, the fevered thrum beating below its surface, tumultuous against the rhythm in his own pounding chest. She filled his senses, incinerating his doubts. There was no room to question. Ollie wrapped her in his arms her, realizing he had ached for this all along. He was hers. He had *always* been hers. Just as she was his. Ayla. *His* Ayla.

He could run no more. This was what he wanted.

This was how Ollie allowed himself to forget.

o   o   o   o

SPOOLING shadows drew Cass closer to her great-grandmother. Though the fixture above the bed still cast its pearlescent glow, it felt as if the light had gone out. The room seemed full and dark, drowned in a thick, unknowable presence. She pulled her cardigan tighter to her shoulders, wishing she had a blanket, wishing she could shake the feeling someone was standing behind her chair.

Gran fell silent. She lay still, eyes closed. Cass had not noticed when she shut them, but it had been a while ago. Since Ollie approached her in the market, at least.

Approached her…

But that had not been Gran, that woman in the market. That was Ayla—the first Ayla—who rejected him. Gran was … was … something else?

This had to be a joke. Yet would even Gran spend her last hours weaving such an elaborate—such a macabre— trick? Age-creased features betrayed no hint of mischief or humour. The old woman looked to be in a dreamless sleep. If not for the minute rise and fall of her chest, Cass might have wondered if she had not already passed.

Cass thumbed the bracelet still in her hands. *Magic.* She hesitated, then slowly, with deliberate care, slipped it on. The weight evaporated from her body, and she lifted infinitesimally off the cradle of her chair. *Magic.* Yanking it off again—settling down with *plunk*—Cass nearly threw the thing across the room. She stopped herself, licking her lips as her gaze returned to the old woman. *There's more to this story. Something's coming.*

WING

"Gran," she whispered, "what happened then? After you arrived in England?" The old woman made no sign of having heard her. "Gran?"

Had she actually fallen sleep? Was she beginning to go? *Oh God.*

Cass reached for her hand. "Please, Gran." Her voice caught in her throat. She blinked at the liquid pressure welling behind her eyes. "Finish the story. Stay and tell me. Unless you're … are you…

"Hush, Cass. I'm not dead. Not yet. I'm just getting a little tired. We're almost done now, but I thought you might need a minute to absorb. Sounds like you did, at that."

There was no mirth in the laugh Cass offered in reply.

"The story goes on though. As all things must. Until Doom comes forward to take us.

"As I said, Ollie allowed himself to forget. For a time, our world was happiness."

o   o   o   o

They lived almost as nomads. Every two or three years, following one opportunity or another, they found themselves boxing up everything and relocating to a new city. One by one, their children arrived into the world—beginning what would become the prodigious Merrill clan—each born in a different town's hospital. They moved from

London to Bristol. From Brighton to Norwich to Leeds. They crossed the Atlantic and spent a year in Boston. Albany. Montreal. Calgary. Landing finally in Victoria, British Columbia.

Until its debt could be satisfied, Qunae contented itself to reside with the family, disguised as a live-in servant. No one ever questioned its presence. "The situation suits me well," it confided to Ollie one evening. Over the years, human and ifrit had negotiated something akin to a friendship. Not *actual* friendship, as Ollie saw it—Qunae was too alien, too unknowable for that—but he felt genuine affection for the magical being, and suspected it harboured similar feelings for him. "I shall be ready when you make your third request; until then, our arrangement allows me to attend business neglected through my imprisonments. It will serve."

For Ollie's part, the idea of making his final wish, of using—and losing—his one remaining miracle was cause for anxiety. Through these happy years, the knowledge he no longer knew he held—that of Ayla's impossible genesis—clung invisibly to his shoulders, weighing on him, dragging him toward his own sunken shadow. One day, he earnestly believed, he would find himself in need of a miracle.

Forgetting had not been easy. Ollie could not simply erase his memories. For years he refused to reflect on them, allowing thoughts to slip over certain moments in his life without ever landing of taking note—like so many eyes he had seen drifting vacantly past Qunae's disguises. Over time, he forgot that he remembered; eventually, he forgot he forgot. Yet the events remained, asleep in the depths of his mind, waiting for a catalyst, just the right trigger, to awaken them.

This came when they crossed the Atlantic.

The voyage was shorter and far more comfortable than their first together. Even so, Ollie was glad as it approached its end. A new life lay ahead; he was eager to meet it.

It was their last night before making land. The children slumbered belowdecks, and he realized a rare opportunity to be alone with his wife. Arm in arm, they watched Heaven's copper disk slide into an endless purple sea. As night's shadows crept inward around twilight's extraordinary hues, Ollie turned, as he so often did, to lose himself in his Ayla's beautiful eyes. Captivated, he stared into the depths of those perfect amber basins. He stared…

…and he gasped.

This moment… Ollie could not understand why his heart had begun to race. *This exact scene…*

He staggered backward. Ayla nearly fell trying to hold him. Something was wrong. He struggled to lay grip to the memory, fought to rip it from his own grasp. *The bridge. I gathered figs for you. But you threw them. You were so angry!* They had scarcely known each other then; what reason could they have had to fight? *And then I wouldn't speak to you—I*

WING

have no idea why—not for weeks. Until ... until... Ollie looked from his wife to the dying sunset. *...Until this. Exactly this moment—one just like it.*

"My love, what's the matter?" Concern raked Ayla's voice, tightened the muscles in her face. Frightened eyes wavered up at him.

No. That was only the surface.

He saw something then which he had never allowed himself to see, though it was infernally familiar. Like it had always been there. Not *in* his wife's eyes. *Behind* them. A flatness, a void. As if her body were hollow.

"Ayla?"

"What, Ollie? What's going on?"

Ollie shook his head. She had *hated* him back then. "Ayla?"

Ayla threw her arms around him, squeezing tight. "Ollie, I'm right *here*! God, what's wrong?" How his face must have looked to earn such a reaction.

Ollie swallowed. He took her by the shoulders and gently detached her. "What—" he began, faltering, struggling to articulate. "Do you ... remember what changed your mind? Back when we met?" His wife's brow crinkled. "You pulled me from the river, remember? I was such a cocky little shit, and you were having none of it. Then on that other bridge... I can't ... I can't remember what I did to change your mind about me. Do you?"

"Ollie, why—"

"Please, darling! Tell me what you remember."

Ayla stepped away from her husband. His hands relaxed, allowing her arms to slip free. She made a careful examination of her shoes. "I wasn't going to… You were so… Then I … I…" Her eyes found his.

Flat.

Empty.

Oh God.

"Go," Ayla said suddenly. Ollie opened his mouth but she gave him no chance to speak. "Go—could you … go look in on the children? Please?" Ollie nodded. Reluctantly, he turned and left her to check after their young ones.

Oliver Merrill adored his wife. Twelve years, they had been together. He knew he could not live without her. But it would never be the same between them again. Ollie had begun to remember.

o   o   o   o

"HE tried to make it work." Gran's voice was weak. "He tried to pretend all this was normal. For the children mostly, I think; they deserved a *real* mother. But for himself too. Even for me—bless his stupid heart—even though he knew I didn't actually feel anything."

"Gran—"

"Hush, my Cass. It's almost time."

Cass's heart had climbed into her throat. Cold sweat dampened her clothes. What was happening? Why would Gran say such things? The old woman continued, oblivious to her great-granddaughter's unease. Her eyes remained closed, her voice little more than a gasp; in the room's silence, it was as loud as any scream.

"Ollie thought he could do it. Even years later, after his memories had fully resurfaced. He thought his love alone might be enough. Of course, it wasn't. Every time he looked at me, he saw it a little clearer—that void inside. Until it was *all* he saw. Probably, he would have grown to hate me. For what I was. For what I *wasn't.* That might have been easier. Only, that darned blessing, you know? By his own wish, his own words, his love couldn't be doused.

"It was hard. We fought. Sometimes he couldn't bring himself to fight—I mean, what was the point?—and he'd leave for a day or two to try and find some perspective. You could say it was difficult for *both* of us … if you didn't know better."

"Gran, what… Why are you saying these th—"

"Quiet, child. You see, Ollie knew he had but one way out. Magic was the net that snared him; only magic could set him free. But he didn't know what blessing to actually beg, and for a long time, he was too scared to consider it. He'd botched two already, remember. What if he messed up the third? It was years before he found the nerve to even

WING

bring the problem to Qunae. But, finally one day, he could bear it no more."

Gran fell silent. Cass waited.

A minute passed.

Two minutes.

Four.

Still, she said nothing.

"Gran? *Gran?*"

The old woman's eyelids opened.

Cass recoiled.

FURY.

There was no emptiness behind those eyes, no lifeless void like in the story. She saw the very look she had convinced herself she imagined. Only worse. It crashed against her, splintering her spirit, squeezing the air from her lungs. She struggled to breathe as the atmosphere crystalized around her.

"I'm sorry," Gran said.

Her voice was thin as parchment.

Her gaze flared like a supernova.

"I think I'm going now. I can't seem to stay awake. But the story's almost done. I can finish. We're almost done, I promise. You see, that was when Ollie made his wish."

CHAPTER TWELVE
The Last Blessing

"I can't keep going. I've tried. So long, I've tried. It's like watching her die each day. Only … she never does. I don't get to mourn her, do I? I just keep *seeing her*, looking into those empty sockets. And … *I* die a little inside. I don't know how much longer I can go on. I don't want to feel this way anymore."

As it so often did when Ollie spoke, the jinni stood pensive for a time, engulfing his words in a tide of silence. "This is what you wish?" it asked when it answered at last. "To love her no more?"

Ollie's brow fell into his palms. "No. Somehow … somehow, that would be worse."

Qunae considered. "I could take her away. Make you forget she ever was."

His head snapped up. "Not an option." For once, he felt certain in his words. His happiness, his whole being, was tied to Ayla's existence, to her presence in his life. Without her—without his love for her—the world would be an empty, bitter place. He needed a solution, just not that one. Softening his voice, he spoke again. "Please, Qunae. Help me. What else can you do?"

The jinni considered. "I can change *you*, make you stop caring what you do, or do not, see in her."

Ollie growled his frustration. He shook his head; needles accompanied the violent motion. Not caring would be as bad as not loving her. As bad as forgetting. He said this aloud. Qunae just sighed.

It was Christmas Eve. Christmas Day now, Ollie supposed, as midnight had come and gone. The children were in bed—all but the eldest who had started university this year and begged to stay at school over the break. Ayla, too, was asleep, upstairs where Ollie knew *he* should be. The prospect of joining her, however, of lying beside her, or in her arms, was more than he could handle.

He had been doing so well, pretending, shuttering the despair that daily threatened to engulf him. He had not argued with his wife in months, had not needed to leave— not needed to escape those empty eyes—in nearly a year. But suddenly, in the glow of tonight's celebration, Ollie felt as if the air were constricting around him, the walls closing in. He felt himself sinking, faster and deeper than ever before. *It isn't going to end*, he despaired, watching his family at play, alive in a joy he could not share. *This will never get better.*

After the children had grown sleepy, and amidst many a loud protest, gone off to bed, after Ayla herself had

117

retired—hiding as best she could the mask of hurt and unease that never failed to slice him open—Ollie was left with
Qunae. And he knew then the time had come. Tonight, he
would beg his final wish.

It was going as poorly as ever he imagined.

"That energy," he whispered hoarsely, "that glint, I just
need to see it when I look at her. Can you-you … instill it
somehow? It doesn't even have to be real; just *paint* it on.
As long as I can see it!"

The jinni snorted. "Nothing I could create would re-
semble what you ask for. Only life can do this. And as I
have said, that is beyond me."

Ollie wiped a knuckle across his face. He was beginning
to hyperventilate. The world blurred around him, and his
knees felt as if they could buckle at any moment. For all
Ayla's unreality, for all the emptiness he saw in her, she was
his life. Knowledge of how bare the foundations on which
that life was built, of how soft the ground beneath, was
physically destroying him. Yet here stood the edifice of his
love, too vast to move, too beautiful to demolish. And here
he stood, trapped within its walls.

In this agitated state, guard down and vulnerabilities
drawn open, the strangest thought slipped into Ollie's
head. *Erbörü, that devil. This is* his *fault.*

The aberrant notion momentarily scattered his miseries.

Erbörü? He blinked. Where had *that* come from? Ollie
had not given thought to the wolf in years; suddenly here

WING

he was, skulking, thief-like, into his mind. *I guess the son of a bitch's found one last victim. Revenge from beyond the grave.* He pictured the beast—he could almost see him—standing as he had in the entrance of the ruin. Hot predatory glare. Slaver glinting orange off those horrible teeth.

That was when all of this began. That was when…

Ollie's breathing slowed.

That's when…

Erbörü *was* a part of this. He was the one who…

Time stopped.

Erbörü. That was his answer. How had it not occurred to him? Strength returned to his limbs. His surroundings snapped back into focus. But would it work? How would Qunae react to such a wish?

"What if…" he began; then he hesitated. *It's the only way. I have to.* "What if *you* inhabit her?" The ifrit cocked its head. Clearly, no such idea had occurred to it. Ollie hurried on. "You've done it before. Only this time, instead of making her bleed fire, you just … just live there, looking out? Would that give her a-a-a life spark? Something I could see?"

Qunae said nothing. At first, Ollie thought it was simply taking its time as it always did, but the silence went on. "Well?" he prodded. "Would it work?"

"Do you know what you ask?" The ifrit's voice was the gnashing hiss of water dropped in a volcano. "Do you have any idea?"

WING

Ollie stiffened his spine. "Would I see life when I looked in my wife's eyes?"

"This thing, Oliver Merrill, would imprison me again—*again!*—after a thousand years bound in scorched clay, after hundreds more trapped in my covenant with the wolf! And you would ask it of me still? You would condemn me to decades, perhaps a *century* of confinement? Do you think time's melody plays any faster to my ear? Do you think I will not chafe with every minute, every *second* of captivity?!"

Ollie retreated a step. The jinni's voice had risen to a thunderous cacophony. He feared the children would wake and cry out in their beds, that Ayla would rush down to see what was happening. But none of them seemed to exist, only the ifrit, eyes blazing as he had not seen since it exploded from the wolf so many years ago.

Ollie had his answer though. Qunae did not lie. If this idea were to fail, it would have simply told him. But it objected. Steeling himself against the immortal's rage, he stepped forward. "Jinni, by your own promise, you owe me one final—"

"Do not do this, Oliver!" Qunae's voice had changed again. It trembled now, wet with fear. "We are *companions*. You are the only mortal I have ever considered friend! Please do not!"

Ollie gulped. Qunae served him; it had always been so. If not for him, the jinni would still be flying over the Turkish countryside, terrorizing farmers. By its own dictates, it owed him. It had promised him whatever he wanted, and *this* was what he wanted. It was *all* he wanted. He needed it.

"I wish for you to obey my command," Ollie said, choosing his words carefully. "You are to reside in the body of my wife—let your divine spark be seen in her for the remainder of a long and healthy life—leaving her to act, speak and exist as she otherwise would—until the time of her death.

"Just … look out through her eyes. Let me see the life in her. This is what I ask."

Qunae seemed to shrink. The jinni closed its eyes and said nothing.

"I wish it," Ollie insisted.

"I have promised you one more blessing." The ifrit spoke so low its voice was almost lost. As the words spilled from its mouth, however, they grew louder. "You have made your request, so I must grant it. I will occupy your wife's body and show you the life you wish to see. I will *imprison* myself for as long as that body lasts—as you say, a *long and healthy life*." It sneered, and Ollie backed away. Though its tone remained calm, the sound had expanded immensely. "But remember, when you gaze into the *living* eyes of the woman-shaped thing I created—*into the soul you have trapped therein*—I … WILL … HAVE … MY … *VENGEANCE*!

121

"WHEN TIME SEES ME FINALLY—*FINALLY*—FREED … I WILL DRAG YOUR WRETCHED SOUL FROM WHATEVER HELL IT HAS FALLEN AND CLEAVE IT INTO *TEN THOUSAND* AGONIZED SHARDS! I WILL HUNT YOUR CHILDREN … AND *THEIR* CHILDREN, UNTO EVERY GENERATION … AND *BURN THEM ALL TO DEATH*! SCORCH THEIR SPIRITS UNTIL ONLY *SCREAMS* REMAIN! YOUR LEGACY, OLIVER MERRILL, WILL … BE … *ASHES*!!"

If Ollie thought the ifrit's voice had changed before, if he believed he had witnessed its rage, he saw now he had but dipped a toe in the ocean of its fury. He tumbled backward. Hot tears burned scars down his face. Qunae's power was too much. He could feel himself blacking out. He pressed his hands to his ears, smearing the ribbons of blood streaming out. Still the words attacked his skull.

"JINN NEVER FORGET. IFRIT *DO NOT FORGIVE*. TAKE COMFORT IN THE HAPPY EXISTENCE YOU HAVE WROUGHT! FOR NESTED WITHIN IT LURKS YOUR DOOM!"

Then it was gone.

No sound. No flash of light. Simply vanished into nothing.

"I take it back," Ollie mumbled feebly. "Qunae, I'm sorry! I take it back!"

No answer came.

It was too late. The blessing had been given, his wish granted. Qunae was gone. *No*, Ollie thought, *not gone. Trapped.*

Ollie had doomed them both. Doomed them all.

Jinn never forget. Ifrit do not forgive.

WING

CHAPTER THIRTEEN
A Promise to Keep

GRAN'S voice had gone hoarse as the last words escaped her lips. Now she lay silent. Cass could see the energy drain out of her. She appeared to shrink, visibly receding into the mattress, the cavity of her thin hospital cover growing wider around a withering frame. Like watching salt poured onto a snail.

"Gran?" Cass whispered. Her vision grew starry as tears glazed her eyes. "Gran?" Myriad emotions tangled within her; she struggled to lay hold of even one she could identify.

The old woman's eyes were closed. *She's fallen asleep*, Cass realized. *She's going*. Gran's breathing came easy now. The wrinkles on her face appeared to smooth.

A chill passed over Cassidy. The air seemed to leave the room.

"…Gran?"

Acknowledgements

ONCE upon a time, writing was a solitary pursuit for me.

Once upon a time, if you had asked me what I was working on, I would have elatedly shouted you a title. No explanation, no context. A single word, offered with enthusiastic indifference to your curiosity.

Since publishing my first book, *Icarus* (available everywhere online), I've found networks of support and encouragement I'd never dreamed of. (Friends and family. Who'd have thought.) In this vein, I'd like to take the opportunity to thank the people who have shown me writing need not occur in a vacuum, who have helped me see—and fill in—some of my blinds spots, people who have propped me up when I found myself canting.

Of course, my mom and dad, who never flagged in their support. Their encouragement has only grown with my commitment to telling stories. *Keep at it* has been the mantra, and so I have.

I'm grateful to Bahareh, who has cheered me on since the day we met, who has both challenged and championed me, and has always been eager to explore new ideas and creations. Her insights rarely fail to surprise me, and our time together has made me both a better writer and a better person.

Glenn is someone who's knowledge and opinions I've come to rely on. I respect and admire him as a writer, as a person, and as a friend. I can't imagine putting a story into the world without first seeking his opinion.

Diana and Dre stand among (if not simply *are*) my best friends. Artistic soul's, both, they have been steadfast comrades through the years, never failing to encourage. So too with my oldest author-friend Brent; my sometimes-writing-partner Lauren; and Karen, my one-woman, live-in discussion group. As well as my fantastic beta readers, Milla, Ann, Ian and Uli. Thank you all.

Of course, *Matriarch* would not be what it is without the beautiful cover created by Dane Low at Ebook Launch (ebooklaunch.com), an absolute pro, and brilliant artist in his own right.

I'm also grateful to the Writing Community on Twitter, which has embraced me, offered endless discussion and support, and helped me spread my works to many who would have never otherwise had a chance to read them. I could name a dozen WC individuals whose presence I've come to value (too many to mention), but in particular I'd like to thank Travis and LadyDay.

Finally, of course, thank *you* for reading my little book. More than anything, my goal is to share stories with the world; in reading my work, you've allowed me to do this. I am grateful—truly, deeply grateful—to you for welcoming me into your life. I hope my words, and any emotions they may have evoked, have been adequate compensation for the opportunity.

Also by Adam Wing

In a time remembered only in myth, on the Isle of Crete, where a brutal king rules absolute, Icarus lives a life of loneliness. Desperate to protect the boy, his father forbids him from even speaking to another human being. But as all children learn to confound their parents, Icarus ventures into a bond of friendship and brotherhood, uncovering powerful emotions he never knew existed ... emotions he has only just begun to understand.

Icarus's connection with the son of his father's enemy sets events into motion that endanger them all. And even as his father plots their escape, death settles around them.

Chased by tragedy, on wings of feathers, wax, and endless promise, the boy and his father make their bid for freedom. Safe at last ... as long as Icarus remembers his father's words...

Also by Adam Wing

APOCA LYPSE SINK SHIPS

Explore the strange, the dark, and the unexpected (and
on occasion, the ridiculous).

This anthology of weird tales will pull you into the hidden
cracks and lost places of human experience. What lurks
beneath the surface? Who are we when the real and the
impossible have become one?

What do we hide from the people around us? Or from
ourselves?

Also by Adam Wing

OLD MAN ON THE BUS
a short story

He boards the bus tonight, like any other night.
After a long, tiring shift he just wants to go home.
But tonight is not like any other.
Tonight he may not make it home at all…

Thanks for reading my novella!

Matriarch was a passion project for me. (I actually walked away from a book I'd started when the idea popped into my head.) It means a lot to be able to share it with you. I hope you enjoyed it, and that it meant something to you too.

If you'd like to learn more about me or my work, please check out my website *www.wingwriting.com* where you'll find info about my writing, travels and life; you'll get to see some of my dumb artwork, read my writing blog (Dog-Eared Corner), and more. Or if you just want to say hi, find me on Twitter at @AdamWingWriting. I'd be delighted to hear from you!

– Adam Wing